A
Harlequin
Romance

OTHER
Harlequin Romances
by JEAN S. MACLEOD

Many of these titles are available at your local bookseller,
or through the Harlequin Reader Service.

For a free catalogue listing all available Harlequin Romances,
send your name and address to:

HARLEQUIN READER SERVICE,
M.P.O. Box 707, Niagara Falls, N.Y. 14302
Canadian address: Stratford, Ontario, Canada.

or use order coupon at back of book.

THE
RAINBOW DAYS

by

JEAN S. MACLEOD

HARLEQUIN BOOKS   TORONTO
WINNIPEG

Original hard cover edition published in 1973
by Mills & Boon Limited

© Jean S. Macleod 1973

SBN 373-01719-7

Harlequin edition published September 1973

Printed in Canada

CHAPTER I

Standing in the departure lounge at Heathrow airport, Vanessa Gilbert thought she would be glad to leave England behind even for the space of three short months. It was February and incredibly cold, but over and above that her life seemed to be at some bleak crossroads where one way was as good as another. Her parents had died within weeks of each other after a car crash and she was virtually alone in the world. There was Sarah, of course, but Sarah was happily married in France and had hurried back there after her father's funeral. 'You'll manage,' she had said. 'You always do.'

When she thought of her sister Vanessa felt curiously numb. They had been so close as children, but marriage had changed Sarah into someone quite different. They had drifted apart and Sarah had quite cheerfully sacrificed one family for the other. It was a long way to come from the South of France except for a special occasion. A funeral, for instance. Afterwards Sarah had left her to manage as best she could, advising her to sell the shabby old house in the Cotswolds and come to London. 'It will be nearer if you ever want to visit us,' she had said, although Vanessa had felt that there was very little real warmth in the invitation. Pierre, Sarah's farmer husband, had a large family of his own to support and she would hardly be welcome at La Moule, except for a day or two.

Well, she had to live with that. Vanessa shook the self-pity from her as she searched the crowd for her new employer. She had been recommended to Alex Rossiter by an old friend of the family, a solicitor practising in Cheltenham who had a London connection and strongly advised her to 'get away for a while'.

Good advice all round, she supposed, thinking of the tall, gaunt man who had interviewed her briefly a month ago and told her that she 'would do'. She had typed and prepared her father's manuscripts for so long that she knew she could give Alex Rossiter good value for his money, but waiting for him now she wondered fleetingly if she had been wise to accept the first job she had been offered. She knew nothing about this man except that he was a highly successful novelist who was going home to the Caribbean to finish his latest book.

They had met briefly three weeks ago in James Balfour's office to discuss a salary and her mode of travel, and finally Alex had decided that they should go together. It was as simple as that. He could trust her to be at the airport in time.

Well, here she was, but where was Alex? She searched the crowd of travellers milling around the departure lounge once more, and then she smiled. To miss Alex Rossiter, even in a crowd, would be almost impossible! He came towards her, the complete extrovert, hung about with the equipment of his trade. He dressed as he wrote, extravagantly, flamboyantly, rarely appearing without a bulging folder of manuscript under his arm. He had come to James Balfour's dignified office in a green corduroy suit and a yellow, open-necked shirt with a purple and white kerchief knotted at his throat, and something of a world which she had only guessed about had come in with him, a freer world than her own, perhaps, and certainly different.

He wore the same suit now with a quieter shirt, but he still disdained a collar and tie, although he admitted to the cold.

'There you are!' he said. 'I knew you wouldn't let me down. I think I've had enough of London in this foul weather. Haven't you?'

He put his portable typewriter down between his feet to examine the sheaf of tickets he held. It was as if they were old friends, as if they had met dozens of times and not just twice before in James Balfour's office. Her heart warmed to him.

'I've got stacks of luggage,' he remarked. 'How about you?'

'I haven't very much.' She indicated her two

6

modest suitcases waiting to be put on the scales. 'I thought I might buy some lighter clothes once we get to Bridgetown.'

He considered her for a moment uncertainly.

'Surely,' he said, thinking of something else. 'Possibly I'm overweight,' he added. 'I generally am. Can you hang on here while I find out?'

She watched him stride across to the nearest weigh-in as if the place belonged to him and saw the heads that were turned as he passed.

'Some celebrity or other, no doubt,' a painted woman in a mink coat remarked as she joined the queue for the departure gate. 'They're all alike, dressing to attract attention!'

Vanessa thought that Alex was more or less discreetly attired this morning, however, and he certainly did not dress to attract attention. This much she knew about him instinctively. He had little use for convention in the strictest sense of the word, living as he did by his own code, and she thought that he hardly noticed the other people as they finally walked out to the big jet which was to carry them to the other side of the world and the sunshine he missed so much.

'Once you've lived in the Caribbean for any length of time,' he told her when they had found their seats, 'you can't settle for long anywhere else. It gets to be in your blood, though recently I've tried to forget that.' He gazed past her to the rainswept tarmac. 'I've lived in Switzerland for the past three years and I still have a house there. Maybe it's the place where I'll finally settle. I just don't know.'

Nor care, she thought. There was an indifference about him which frankly puzzled her.

'How long is it since you've been home?' she ventured.

'Funny you should say that,' he mused. 'Home! I suppose it is, after all.' He shifted in his seat, fastening his safety-belt as they began to taxi along the runway. 'I haven't been back there for some time. This will be my first visit to La Sola for over three years.'

She was conscious of surprise because he had spoken

7

of their destination with warmth.

'Your family will be looking forward to seeing you,' she remarked.

'Most of them will.' He smiled wryly. 'My mother takes the view that I've deserted La Sola, but she'll be glad to see me back there, even if it isn't for good. Tom—he's my youngest brother—was away at school when I left, but he'll be grown now—all of sixteen years old, in fact. Or is it seventeen?' He made a rapid mental calculation. 'Seventeen, it is! The years fairly slip away.'

'Is that all the family?' Vanessa asked.

He shook his head, frowning at the wet tarmac.

'There's Max,' he said almost reluctantly.

'Is he older than you?'

'No—younger.'

There was a silence.

'You don't get on very well,' she suggested.

Alex laughed.

'That might be the understatement of the year,' he declared. 'Nobody is expected to " get on " with Max, least of all me. He's a law unto himself, as we all are, I suppose. Max owns everything within sight on the island now, I understand—a worthy citizen—but when he was younger people called him Henry Morgan. He was an absolute pirate in those days. He took what he wanted. It was his way, because material things mattered to him.'

His voice dropped on an unexpected note of uncertainty, as if he didn't quite believe that last statement of his, as if his final assessment of his brother might well be to come.

'You haven't met for some time?' She asked the question for something to say, aware that his thoughts were scarcely happy ones.

'Three years.' The admission came with absolute certainty this time, as if their last encounter was etched all too sharply on Alex's memory. 'He practically turned me off the island.'

She felt shocked.

'But now all is forgiven?'

8

'Not all.' He was equally sure of that. 'But my mother is ill—seriously ill—and Max thinks I should spend some time with her. This is the only way.' He looked down at the bulging briefcase laid across his knees. 'I must work, but at least I can finish my book at La Sola.'

'Perhaps your brother could find you something to do on the island afterwards?' Vanessa suggested.

An angry colour stained his cheeks.

'He wouldn't try, and I really don't want to grow cocoa or sugar or even pineapples,' he said. 'I made up my mind about that long ago.'

She wanted to ask him if he was married or if the piratical Max had helped himself to a wife, but decided against such an intimate question, believing that he might vouchsafe the information himself. Alex, however, turned the conversation to her own background and she found herself answering his questions until the lunch trays were handed round.

'Your father wrote mainly text-books,' he mused, 'but I don't suppose typing my sort of stuff will be much different. You needn't bother to check my facts,' he grinned. 'I do a lot of research before I begin.'

'Jimmy Balfour said this was your fourth novel.' She was eager to hear about his work. 'I've read two of them and liked them very much,' she added shyly.

'Nice of you to say so.' He gave her a friendly smile. 'Not everybody does, but they go on selling, and that's the main thing.' He drew a deep breath. 'Three novels and as many plays, all of them remarkably successful,' he mused. 'Where does that get one?'

'Surely you're not grumbling?'

'No, indeed! I make a fair living,' he admitted, 'but what I want to know is—does it count? I'm no genius—I recognise that—but I'd like to do just one good book before I die. Something that would hit them between the eyes, make them see—'

He broke off as the hostess came with their trays, reverting automatically to his former good-natured approach as he transferred the briefcase to the over-head rack.

'Maybe this one will shake 'em rigid,' he decided. 'It's odd how the current opus always seems to be better than anything that's gone before. Maybe you'll bring me luck,' he added.

'I don't think you need a great deal of luck, as you mean it,' she told him. 'You are very successful, and you seem happy enough.'

He turned to help her with her tray.

'I wonder if you'll be happy at La Sola,' he said unexpectedly.

'Why shouldn't I be? I'm there to do a job of work and I believe I can do it to your satisfaction.'

'So long as you can type!'

'I went to college to learn. I also took languages and can keep accounts.'

'You're a font of learning,' he acknowledged, biting into a bread roll. 'Don't let Max spirit you away from me to keep his accounts at La Sola, though. It's the sort of thing he would do if he thought he needed you.'

'The complete pirate, in fact?'

'I guess so.'

His mouth was suddenly compressed and she found herself wondering if there was bad blood between the brothers, some old sore which still festered in spite of the passing years.

Alex ordered her a rum drink.

'You must get acclimatised,' he said.

'Tell me about the island.' She turned towards him eagerly. 'There's so much I want to know.'

He described his home in words so poetic that she had no longer any doubt about his literary ability nor about his love for La Sola. Why then had he left it? For experience, perhaps, which is every man's prerogative, or was it because of Max? She could not get the thought of his brother out of her mind.

Alex explained about the time lapse during their journey, which she knew about but had never experienced, and by the time they had reached Bermuda her pulses had quickened with a new expectancy. This was something she had dreamed about many times, all these magic islands lying down there below her on a sea of incredible blue: she watched the water breaking on the golden cays and the sun glinting on strange, jagged peaks, drawing in a swift breath of excitement, and a wild rose colour stained her cheeks, making Alex Rossiter realise how lovely she really was. Like an excited child on a wished-for holiday, he decided—utterly unspoiled.

The final destination of the few passengers who got off at Nassau was probably Miami Beach, but Vanessa did not envy them. Her own destination seemed far more exciting, more personal now that she had Alex's word-picture to colour it for her.

Another meal was served, but there was land beneath them now, dotted on the brilliant blue of the Atlantic, and she hardly noticed what she ate. Alex read for a while, but Vanessa could not take her eyes from the shifting scene beneath them. Island after island came and disappeared, all the long chain of the Bahama cays spread out in the sun intersected by a thousand narrow channels where little ships plied their trade or glided idly from one small port to the next in search of pleasure and, she supposed, freedom.

There was more land away to the west, hazy and mountainous, but soon the islands began to appear again.

'We're coming up to the Virgins now,' Alex said, bending over her to get his bearings. 'Down there! You can see them all to-day, doing their best to charm us! Some people think they're the most beautiful, but they can't really compare with the Grenadines. You'll understand what I mean when we get there. Antigua is beautiful, too, but it's gradually being spoilt. We used to put in at Falmouth in the old days when we went up and down the chain on holiday. My father kept a schooner, just for the love of it, and we all learned to sail before the mast!'

He was speaking a lot about his youth, about the days before he had left the island to seek his fortune as a writer in another land.

'After Barbados,' she asked, 'what then?'

He hesitated.

11

'We should be met,' he said uncertainly. If not, we can go out with the steamer or on one of the freighters. Tomorrow or the day after. You ought to see Barbados.'

'I'll have to keep reminding myself that I'm a working girl!'

'It needn't be all work.' He moved a little nearer. 'I'm not a slave-driver, Vanessa. You'll have time off, and I hope I can show you the Islands at their best.'

'They're bewitching enough even from this distance. I had no idea there were so many—dozens and dozens of them, "pointed and peaked"!'

'They're the tops of a mountain chain,' he told her. 'The tips of a lost continent, and many of them are volcanic.'

'Soufrière and Pelée,' she remembered. 'I've read about them.'

'They were major eruptions,' Alex explained. 'We have our own resident volcano at La Sola, but he only groans once in a while to convince us he's still there. They're a sleepy lot these days, but there's something about a volcano which fires the imagination, whether it's active or not. All that fire and rage slumbering beneath the surface and nothing showing. Max is like that,' he added thoughtfully. 'Dark and calm outwardly, but smouldering underneath all the time, ready to explode. He used to wish that our volcano would erupt, just for the hell of it, but that was one thing he wasn't able to direct. That and—'

Again he seemed to draw his thoughts up, reserving the admission for a later day perhaps, and soon they were flying towards a larger island, coming in to Barbados with the sun glinting on the wing beneath them in an arc of rainbow light and all the wide Caribbean sea stretching westward to infinity.

The giant airliner went down like a gentle bird, its landing wheels touching twice before they made final contact with the land.

'I can't believe I'm really here!' Vanessa gasped. 'It all looks, so—fabulous.'

'You'll only realise what the Islands are really like

after you have lived here for a while,' Alex declared, unfastening his seat-belt. 'They cast a spell which you'll never be able to forget.'

'Yet you came away,' she reminded him,

His pleasant mouth took on a more determined line.

'I'm going back,' he said.

'Then you do mean to stay—with your brother's permission?'

'With or without Max's permission, if I choose,' he answered.

She wondered if his brother would come to meet them, and hoped not. Maxwell Rossiter was too controversial a character for her to feel truly at ease in his presence, she imagined.

'He could have changed, though,' Alex mused, almost as if he had read her thoughts. 'I wouldn't know.'

'Three years can be a long time,' Vanessa suggested.

'Not on the island, and Max always had a thing about La Sola. He wanted it, while I didn't, at that time.'

'And now?' she felt compelled to ask.

'I don't know,' he confessed as they stood up to collect their hand-luggage. 'I just don't know. Maybe I should put down roots somewhere nearer home than Switzerland. Maybe I've been a wanderer on the face of the earth for too long.'

She could sense the tension in him which had something to do with his brother, yet it was impossible to guess what it could be. And she was not really concerned, she tried to assure herself. Alex Rossiter had employed her for three months until he had finished his book and then he would have no further use for her services. It was a purely business proposition and she accepted it as such, although the fact that she was bound for an unknown destination with this man, going to a remote Caribbean island where he had run free as a boy, was bound to stir her pulses just a little.

She looked across the seats at him, assessing him frankly, the deep lines etched on his handsome face, the level gaze, the eyes smoke-grey, rarely serious, the

13

smiling, mobile mouth, yet somewhere she detected the hint of tragedy.

'So?' he asked. 'What have you decided? You've been studying me long enough.'

Confused, she looked beyond him.

'I was being rude.'

'Summing me up? I don't think so. You've taken me on trust so far. You have every right to ask a few questions.'

'I was wondering about your mother,' Vanessa told him. 'How will she feel about having a stranger thrust upon her when she has been ill?'

'You needn't worry about my mother,' Alex assured her. 'She takes most things in her stride, and being ill isn't going to alter that.' He sat down again with the briefcase across his knees, waiting for the doors to be opened, and she saw the quick shadow which passed across his face. 'I was her oldest son and I failed her,' he added briefly.

'In what way?'

'Oh, dozens of ways, I expect. She had no use for an artist in the family, for one thing. She was obsessed by La Sola, especially after my father died, and her determination to keep it in the family made me a natural thorn in her flesh, I guess.'

It was obvious that he admired his mother, but perhaps he did not love her.

'Is she—fond of Max?'

He thought about it.

'They're alike in a good many ways,' he decided at last. 'When my mother makes a decision she sticks to it, and if it proves disastrous she doesn't moan. Max is like that, too, although maybe he's not over-anxious to admit his failures. He's arrogant in that respect, I suppose, and maybe he's had luck on his side. A lot of luck.'

She thought again about Maxwell Rossiter, wondering what his immediate reaction would be to her arrival at La Sola, and then she laughed outright. As if he would be even remotely interested!

'You're amused?' Alex asked.

14

'It was nothing. I just wondered how your brother will react to me. He doesn't sound the sort of person who likes a woman cluttering up the place.'

'That will be for my mother to decide,' Alex said firmly. 'After all, she's still the head of the family, whatever Max may think.'

Vanessa could picture his mother very well. She would be a tall, commanding, eagle-eyed woman demanding unequivocal obedience from her sons where La Sola was concerned, and perhaps that was why she and Alex had never seen eye to eye. Yet there seemed to be something else, a further reason for the reticence which appeared to exist between mother and son.

Alex was no time in finding a taxi, while she stood completely enchanted by the amenities of the island airport. The flowers in their colourful profusion were a revelation to her, while above her head shone the sun clear and golden, in a cloudless blue sky. Tempered by the trade winds which 'blew home' into Bridgetown, there was nothing sultry about the heat which beat on her skin, nothing of the languor she had expected when she had first seen this lovely green island lying beneath her on the silky water of the Caribbean Sea. Her pulses leapt with pleasurable anticipation. Even though this was not a holiday on which she was embarking, there would be time for lying in the sun, time to feel the caress of that blue water on her body, time, perhaps, to stand and stare.

They were first off on the long, straight road which led to the capital. Alex certainly knew the ropes, and the taxi driver grinned at him in evident appreciation.

'You come here often,' he guessed, showing his magnificent white teeth in a wide, friendly grin.

'I belong here,' Alex answered with satisfaction.

Bridgetown surprised Vanessa.

'What did you expect?' he asked her.

'Oh—a town, certainly, but not like this.' Vanessa's eyes were everywhere. 'I suppose I hardly expected so many palatial shops and all this activity going on, as if we hadn't just driven through sugar cane!'

He smiled at that.

' I thought you wanted to go on a spending spree,'
he challenged.

' I'll need something cool to wear, but if you had
other things in mind—' She hesitated.

' I'll put you down in Roebuck Street,' he decided.
' Then you can walk down to the Square. Trafalgar
Square! That should keep you thinking of home!'

' I've already forgotten London,' she confessed.
'This is heavenly!'

There were flowers everywhere, exotic blooms she
had only seen previously in the windows of expensive
florists. They tumbled over garden fences and fes-
tooned old wooden porches in the approaches of the
city, and larger houses gazed at her over their confining
walls, square and elegant, with broad stone porticos
and latticed balconies clinging to their pink stucco
sides and more flowers tumbling in abundance from
decorative urns flanking the wooden doorways which
led to the street.

Children ran beside the kerb, calling to one another
and laughing, their dark, shining faces turned to the
sun. It was a day for laughter, Vanessa thought.

' I have to see a man,' Alex explained vaguely as he
put her down in what appeared to be one of the main
shopping streets. ' Work your way down to the Square
when you're ready. You can't go wrong, and I'll pick
you up at the corner of Broad Street in an hour.'

It was foolish of her to feel deserted, Vanessa
thought, and perhaps it was only Alex's exuberance
which was at fault. Escorted by him all the way from
London, she had had nothing to do but absorb all the
new impressions which crowded in upon her, but she
should have been prepared to be left alone for an hour.
Their agreement was entirely a business one and she
had shopped on her own in a busy town many times
before.

It was easy enough to find all she needed in the well-
stocked emporiums on either side of the street, for the
whole town seemed to be stuffed with merchandise of
one kind or another. She bought two cotton dresses,
both very gay, the sort of thing that might have looked

16

garish even in an English summer but was so right here under the tropic sun, and then she filled in what time she had left gazing at the bazaars. The Bajan work fascinated her: baskets and bowls and things made from straw or tortoiseshell, and she stood for a long time admiring them. There were little pottery figures standing under palm trees with baskets of fruit on their heads in greens and blues, hand made from the local clay, and bright, attractive ceramic jewellery in fused glass which held all the light of the island in its colourful depth. She could hardly believe that she had left London only that morning under a grey and lowering sky.

Avoiding the more expensive boutiques with their pretty, imported play-clothes and gay Pucci shirts, she bought a head-scarf and a pair of straw sandals further down the street. She had crossed an intersection into another broad highway, but she could already see an open space ahead of her and felt that she was going in the general direction of the Square.

Glancing at her watch, she saw that she still had ten minutes to spare. It was still warm, but there were signs that some of the shops were about to close. Shutters had appeared and assistants came out to gossip on the doorsteps now that the stream of shoppers had thinned. Vanessa would dearly have loved a cup of tea, but did not know where to go. Instead, she paused by yet another bazaar, her attention caught by a lovely necklace of pendant glass lying on a blue silk cushion at the front of the window. The fused glass was beautiful in itself, but the intricate work which had been put into the necklace made it a thing of great beauty.

Gazing at it in admiration, it was a second or two before she realised that she was being watched. Someone standing in the arcaded entrance to the shop was studying her intently. She raised her eyes from the glittering bauble on the cushion to encounter a man's concentrated stare. He was a tall man, deeply tanned, as if all his life had been spent in the open air under this magnificent sun, and his penetrating gaze challenged hers with an open curiosity. The eyes were deep-set, with a glint of fire in them as the light caught them, and although he was conventionally enough dressed in an open-necked shirt and light-coloured slacks the look of the brigand was unmistakable. Perhaps it was the blue kerchief knotted at his throat which heightened the impression, but it certainly had the power to disconcert her for a moment. Then, abruptly, he turned away, as if dismissing her. She watched the tall, lean figure striding off through the thickening crowd of homegoing Barbadians, conscious of an odd sense of impact which she was not likely to forget in a hurry.

Somewhere near a clock struck the hour and she hurried towards Trafalgar Square. Alex was there, waiting for her at the corner of Broad Street as he had promised.

'You're out of breath,' he chided, relieving her of her parcels.

'I didn't want to keep you waiting.' It was true, but her breathlessness had also something to do with that odd encounter with a stranger only a few minutes ago.

'Max is in town,' Alex said.

'You've met?'

He shook his head.

'I got the information from the family solicitor,' he explained. 'I went to see him about—another matter.' He guided her across the Square, his hand firm under her elbow. 'How about some tea?'

'I'm gasping!' she confessed.

He found a hotel overlooking the Square, but he seemed distracted by his own thoughts as she poured their tea.

'Is something wrong?' she asked.

'I've just had a piece of unexpected news which might change my plans a bit.' He dismissed his preoccupation with a shrug. 'Where were we? Talking about Max. We can't flatter ourselves that he's come to meet us, but we might be able to beg a lift if he's going back to the island immediately. It would save

18

us waiting for the steamer, which doesn't go out till to-morrow,' he explained.

' How would you find him?' She was remembering the size of Bridgetown and the crowds gathering in its busy thoroughfares for the homeward trek.

' He'll be at the Careenage loading up for the trip home,' Alex decided. ' Max doesn't waste time in bars or what have you, even for the odd drink. He carries his liquor with him.'

' You sound as if you meant bootleg stuff!'

' I wouldn't be surprised, though he could have changed.' He began to gather up her parcels. ' How much have you spent?'

' Not a lot. I was strong-willed enough to avoid the smart places!'

' Most things are cheap here,' he said, paying the bill. ' Or they used to be. We came over from the island about once a month to do our shopping, so perhaps you'll have to be content with that. No more spending sprees or bright lights for you for the next four weeks or so. How do you feel about it?'

' I won't mind at all. I've come prepared to work.'

' Good!' He looked at her thoughtfully. ' I wouldn't call you beautiful,' he said. ' Just easy on the eye!'

' Whatever made you think of that?' she laughed.

' Because I hadn't really been thinking before. What age are you, Vanessa?'

' Twenty-three.'

' As much as that?' There was a note of banter in his pleasant voice. ' I'm nudging thirty. An age for settling down.'

She did not ask him again if he meant to settle in the Caribbean, but she could not think of a lovelier place, and it was his home. But something had happened there to send him wandering around the world and it still disturbed him.

A short walk across the Square brought them to the Careenage. Alex led the way across the bridge to Bay Street, scanning the rows of craft anchored in the harbour. There were more yachts than Vanessa had ever seen before and two magnificent cruise ships, like great white swans, lying against the wharf. It was the schooners, however, which drew and held her interest with their slender, graceful lines and long bowsprits and their bobbing masts making a forest of the waterfront.

'I'll have to ask,' Alex said. 'One of them will be Max's, but which?' He turned to a young Negro leaning against the wall. 'You know Mr Rossiter's boat?' he asked.

There was instant response.

'Yes, sir! She down there.' The boy pointed to the row of schooners. 'The *Carmelita*. I shure like to go work on that boat, man, but I no' clever enough fo' Mr Rossiter. He big man in Islands; he need good hands to run dem schooners, so help me!'

Alex thanked him.

'So Max is a big man in the Islands now,' he mused as they turned on to the jetty. 'I might have expected something of the kind.'

He sounded faintly cynical and Vanessa decided to let the reference to his brother pass. Her pulses were already stirring to the excitement of their adventure, of going to sea in one of those graceful ships with their tall masts raking the sky and the gentle Caribbean swell washing against their hulls.

By the look of the *Carmelita* she was certainly a seaworthy ship. Rocking gently to the slight swell as the tide came in, she looked the perfect mode of travel in these romantic waters, a natural daughter of that blue and placid sea.

There was no one on board. Alex put his foot on the gangplank and hollered 'Max!' to no avail. Not even the head of a seaman appeared at the open hatch to ask what they wanted, although the schooner itself was impeccable, with its holystoned deck gleaming in the westering sun and its white sails neatly tied along the twin booms. Even to Vanessa's inexperienced eye it had obviously been meticulously restored to its original state for use by its present owner, a thing of which to be justifiably proud. Nothing had been overlooked, from the glistening paintwork on its black

20

topsides to the shimmering streak of the red waterline which lay reflected in the still water of the basin. She could imagine the *Carmelita* gliding gracefully across the bay with the wind in the rigging, breasting the swell like a thoroughbred while Alex—or Max Rossiter—stood at the helm.

'We'll go aboard,' Alex said. 'No use waiting to be asked.'

Their luggage had been left at the hotel for convenience in case the *Carmelita* had already sailed, and after a while Alex looked along the quay with a first sign of impatience.

'Max ought to be on board by now if he means to catch this tide,' he explained, 'and there's no sign of a crew. I'll go back to the hotel and collect our luggage. You wait here and make yourself comfortable. I think I know where I can find Max.'

Vanessa sat on the sun-warmed deck watching the crew of a neighbouring ship as they loaded a cargo of crates and sacks into the hold. They looked at her slightly askance, as if she were an intruder as, no doubt, she was, but it was delightful here on the sunny deck with a soft wind fanning her cheeks and the slap of the sheets against the mast making a soothing music in her ears. Its soporific quality almost lulled her to sleep as she stretched out with her eyes half closed, allowing her thoughts to drift. There was still a great deal of warmth in the sun, but her day had been very long and full of new experiences.

A sudden shadow came between her and the warmth and she looked up to find the man from the bazaar looming over her, legs astride on his own deck. She knew, without having to be told, that this was Maxwell Rossiter.

'What the devil are you doing here?' he demanded.

Alex's eyes were smoke-grey, but these eyes had the flash of steel in them. Both Rossiter eyes, but with a difference.

'I—Alex has gone in search of you.' She stumbled over her explanation, disconcerted by his black frown. 'I wanted to go with him, but I suppose he thought

I was tired.'

'Picking up trinkets in Roebuck Street?' He did not smile. 'What are you to my brother, may I ask?'

She flushed at the barely disguised innuendo.

'I'm acting as his secretary.'

'For want of a better word?'

'I find that grossly insulting!' She tilted her chin proudly. 'I'm here to type your brother's latest novel, but apart from that—'

'Apart from that?' he prompted, waiting.

'There's nothing between us.'

His steady scrutiny said that he didn't believe her. She struggled to her feet, infuriated.

'If you wish me to get off your ship, Mr Rossiter, I shall be only too happy to oblige,' she offered. 'I should have remembered that one waits to be invited aboard.'

'So long as you remember in future,' he said, turning from her.

The native crew were coming aboard from their visit to the town, burdened by their various purchases. Dark, surreptitious glances were directed towards her and turned immediately to the captain of the ship. Maxwell Rossiter barked an order, which was immediately obeyed.

Vanessa walked across the gangplank, hoping that Alex would come, pacing the cobbles with an urgency that showed. This was intolerable—this man making her feel at a loss like this, making her feel a trespasser, unwanted on his ship, at least. Maxwell Rossiter came to the gangplank.

'You'd better step aboard,' he said. 'If Alex has gone to Hinks Street he might be some time.'

'He went in search of you,' she informed him, standing her ground on dry land. 'I'll wait till he gets back, thank you.'

'You'd be more comfortable in the cabin.' He indicated the main companionway. 'We don't smell of dried fish or stale rum, you know. This is a charter vessel when I'm not using her, so I can assure you that everything is ship-shape and Bristol fashion down below.'

'I'll wait,' Vanessa said stubbornly because she felt that he was laughing at her now.

He shrugged his shoulders and went off along the deck, issuing orders, apparently forgetting her. In a few minutes he might be ready to sail and she had half a notion that he would leave her and Alex stranded in Barbados without compunction. She looked up at the rigging and the loosened sails. Where was Alex? Surely there had been time and to spare for him to get to the hotel and back with their luggage.

A taxi rumbled across the bridge and pulled up beside her. Thankfully she watched her employer get out and pay the driver. Their luggage was deposited on the quay. Alex walked towards her, but he was looking beyond her at the schooner and the tall, dark-visaged man pacing the deck.

The brothers faced each other across the gangplank and Alex offered a tentative smile.

'Well, Max,' he said, 'it's been a long time.'

Vanessa did not look at Maxwell Rossiter, but she knew that his face was closed and unsmiling. He pretended not to see his brother's outstretched hand.

'Mother told you we were coming, of course,' said Alex.

'I was sent to meet you.' Maxwell Rossiter's voice was studiedly impersonal. 'You needn't have gone in search of me.'

'I wasn't sure,' Alex said, still on the defensive. Then, remembering his manners, he drew Vanessa forward. 'This is my secretary, Miss Gilbert—Vanessa Gilbert. I have a book to finish.'

Maxwell Rossiter stood aside.

'Come aboard,' he said. 'I've already invited Miss Gilbert, but she preferred to wait for you. Perhaps she was afraid I might abduct her.'

The two men confronted each other with naked animosity in their eyes for a second, and then Alex signalled Vanessa to walk ahead of him on to the deck. Maxwell Rossiter gave another order and their luggage was lifted from the quay.

When will you sail?' Alex asked.

'In half an hour. The tide will be right then.'
His brother escorted them to the main companionway.
'You'll find everything you'll need down there.
It should be a calm crossing.' He glanced briefly in
Vanessa's direction. 'You don't need to worry.'

'He knows what a rotten sailor I am,' Alex said
lightly as he helped Vanessa down the companionway.
'I never could stand a schooner pitching and rolling
all over the place in a bad sea.'

'It looks so absolutely calm,' Vanessa answered,
trying not to think of Max. 'How long does the
crossing take?'

'We should be there by morning, unless we have a
change of wind,' Alex calculated. 'By noon, at the
latest.'

'Does that mean we're going under sail all the
way?'

'Max thinks it's the only way to go,' Alex answered.
'I believe he has an engine in some of his yachts
because of the charters, but he doesn't really approve
of power boats. He believes in sail for sail's sake,
which could be the buccaneer in him raising an ugly
head. Who knows?'

Something had shaken his habitual confidence,
making him unsure of himself for the first time, and
Vanessa's thoughts had no great distance to travel to
Maxwell Rossiter for a reason.

Down in the cabin the shadows rippled along the
bulkheads, playing on the rich red mahogany in a
pattern of light and shade. The sun would linger for
a time in these pleasant waters before it went down
abruptly behind the horizon, and Vanessa planned to
be on deck again to watch her first Caribbean sunset.

Their luggage had been deposited in their respective
cabins with the doors left open for easy identification,
and she found hers next to Alex's, with a firmly-closed
door facing them. The master's cabin, no doubt!
It disconcerted her to know that Maxwell Rossiter
would be so near.

'Come up on deck when you're ready,' Alex called

to her as he passed. 'Bridgetown is well worth a parting glance.'

She washed hurriedly in the small covered hand-basin and took a coat in case the evening breezes might turn chilly later on. She had no idea when they would eat or if they would retire early or late, but somehow she thought that Maxwell Rossiter might stay at the wheel all night. The man in command.

Alex was standing at the rail when she reached the deck and he made way for her beside him. Two Negro sailors were about to release the warps fore and aft, and suddenly there was a movement beneath their feet as the slender bowsprit paid off.

The schooner gathered momentum immediately under a brisk wind off the land and the boom swung out as the heavy mainsail was raised. Maxwell Rossiter issued brisk commanding orders from the bridge. He seemed different now, part of the ship and at one with the elements, his eyes steady on the way ahead as the schooner hurried across the Bay. The effortless grace of this lovely bird of the sea was a joy and contentment to the man, and he seemed to have forgotten them completely.

Vanessa watched in silence as Bridgetown's maze of warehouses and shops receded into the background and was finally lost to view. They were heading straight into the sunset, sailing due west on the mysterious Caribbean Sea, and somewhere out there was La Sola and Max Rossiter's island. That was how she thought of it, even then.

'You'll see Bequia and Mustique first,' Alex promised her. 'The Windwards are fantastic islands. Trouble is, more and more people are finding it out as time goes by, apparently. I'll see a difference in La Sola, too, I should imagine. It would be too much to expect it to have stood still, even for three years. I know Max has built a new harbour and there are one or two houses on the beach, apart from the village proper. We have our own bay, though. Mother would hate it if she had to share La Sola with anyone.'

'Has she lived there all her life?' Vanessa asked,

trying once more to picture Mrs Rossiter as the mother of two such utterly different sons.

' All her married life,' Alex answered. ' She came from Antigua, where her father was a Government official. In those days marrying into sugar was to be commended.'

' But not now?'

He shrugged.

' It still pays, up to a point, but the old private estates are dwindling fast. The consortiums have taken over in a big way and most estates are mixed now, growing cocoa or fruit or bananas as well as sugar. La Sola wasn't big enough to be swallowed up, but it had its own problems of transport, for example, till Max took over.'

She thought of him being the oldest son, but he made no further reference to La Sola and they watched the flying fish in silence for several minutes until the whole sea and the sky above it turned to gold and then to vivid flame.

Vanessa had never seen such a sunset. It blazed across the horizon from end to end, bathing the sea and the schooner and their watching faces in a radiant light. It was impossible to define the colours as they merged into each other, with great shafts of light shooting up into the turquoise sky above their heads.

Spellbound, she gazed at it until it began to fade. The colours paled and a distant band of cloud appeared to rest on the horizon like a mystic island conjured up from the depths of the sea. It brought a sudden coldness to the night and, involuntarily, she shivered, drawing her woollen coat about her as she turned to see Maxwell Rossiter approaching along the deck.

' You can have an early meal,' he offered. ' I dare say you'll be tired.'

' Not unduly,' Alex answered for them both. ' Will you join us? I haven't had a chance to ask you about the family yet.'

Vanessa saw Max stiffen.

' I gather you came because Mother was ill,' he said

briefly. 'She hae good days and bad. You'll probably see a change in her, although the fact that you're here will make a difference.'

Alex shifted his position at the rail.

'And Robin?' he asked.

'Growing apace.' Max's voice was thin. 'I believe he writes to you.'

'Occasionally, under Mother's tuition.' Alex stared down at the darkening sea. 'What about Tom?' he asked.

'He goes to Cambridge at the end of the summer.'

'I'm glad,' Alex said. 'He was always the studious one.'

'I'm not quite sure that he likes the idea,' Max was looking straight ahead. 'He's very fond of La Sola, but he ought to go. He ought to take his chance in the outside world. There's little for him to do here.'

'You seem to be doing all right,' Alex observed.

'I'm different,' Max said immediately. 'Always have been.'

Alex laughed. He seemed to be more relaxed now, yet Vanessa was increasingly aware of the animosity between the brothers who had been brought up together and must have shared a love of the island in their youth. Alex had left the Caribbean far behind him in the past few years, while Max had remained faithful to La Sola, but that was not the whole story. Max's antagonism went deeper than a younger son's resentment at being left to support the family home while his older brother roamed the world. It was more personal, not something between La Sola and Alex or La Sola and Max. It was between brother and brother, and she felt that nothing would ever erase it.

'We could have come over with the steamer,' Alex said, 'but I didn't feel inclined to trust myself to Albert Talg's piraque, even in this weather.'

'You're behind the times,' Max informed him briefly. 'Albert Talg is dead. I have the sole concession now.'

Alex looked surprised.

'I never thought of you as a business man,' he said. 'Times change, apparently.'

'People also change,' Max reminded him. 'You'll see a difference in most things once you get to the island.'

He left them to go down to the cabin, where their meal had been set out. It surprised Vanessa to see that they were to be served by a white-coated steward, but no doubt that was all part of the chartering side of Max's business. There were only two places set, each with a formidable array of cutlery. Max would not be joining them.

There was no pleasure in his acceptance of her, Vanessa realised, remembering how brusquely he had told them to 'come aboard'. She knew that the traditional invitation from a ship's captain was 'welcome aboard', but she was Alex's guest and she would not let herself be intimidated by his brother. Nothing Maxwell Rossiter could do or say would influence her once she had come this far. She was determined to see her job through, as she had promised, in spite of his obvious disdain. With a bit of luck, he might not be at La Sola for any length of time. Hadn't Alex referred to him as a brigand, so his natural habitat would be the sea.

She had to admit that he looked every inch the mariner as he stood there at the wheel with his dark face turned to the sky, and it was not very long before she realised what a poor sailor Alex was. Long before the last course was served he had pushed his plate aside.

'I've had enough,' he said. 'I'll turn in now, if you don't mind.'

He was very pale, although the movement of the ship hadn't altered.

'Is there anything I can do for you?' she asked. 'Anything I can get you?'

'Not a thing!' He attempted a smile. 'I'm always like this at sea. Have to get my head down—or else!'

'Perhaps, if I asked your brother—'

'He'd only laugh at you. Max has never been seasick in his life. He thinks it's effeminate.'

'Don't worry about me,' she said when he didn't move towards his cabin immediately. 'I'll be all right. I'll turn in, too, in a little while. It's been a very long day.'

'Longer than most.' He grinned at her. 'If you go on deck again, take your coat,' he warned.

She thought that he left her reluctantly. If they hadn't been at sea he would have stayed talking until long after midnight and perhaps she would have learned a little more about him. They could have discussed his book and what he hoped to make of it, for one thing.

The steward brought her coffee and she stood drinking it beside the open companionway. Above her the cobalt blue sky glittered with a million stars, some so near that she felt she could have touched them if she had stretched out her hand. The night wind was warm, blowing in on her face, and suddenly she wanted more than anything else to go on deck.

Why not? It wasn't yet ten o'clock and she could keep well away from the bridge and any chance encounter with Maxwell Rossiter.

Taking her coat from the hook behind her cabin door, she paused to listen for a moment at Alex's. He was faintly snoring.

On deck the sea seemed very near and the stars nearer still. Their faintly diffused light illuminated the water and the upperstructure of the schooner itself, etching the twin masts and the gently billowing sail in silver. She leaned on the rail to look down at the surging waves. The swell had increased and the *Carmelita* pitched rhythmically, dipping her long bowsprit to the sea. The sound of the wind in the rigging and the swish of the advancing waves blurred all other sound until a man spoke at her elbow.

'You seem to enjoy the sea, Miss Gilbert,' Maxwell Rossiter observed. 'Are you a seasoned traveller?'

'Not at all.' She turned to face him and saw his

eyes glitter in the starlight. ' This is my first experience on a sailing ship.'

' You weather it well,' he said. ' My brother isn't so keen.'

' Poor Alex ! ' she sympathised. ' It must be dreadful to feel so ill.'

He looked beyond her at the sea.

' On a night like this it's a shame to be down below,' he said.

The wind was freshening and she felt the ship lurch towards it as a rush of dark water ran along the port. Max Rossiter watched her with interest, expecting her to go below. Instead, she held on to the rail with both hands, looking fixedly at the stars. They were almost too brilliant for belief, glittering above the mastheads like a myriad tiny lamps backed by the velvet of the night sky. There was a magic about the Caribbean scene that twisted her heart, making her wish that she need never go away. Restlessly she sighed.

' How long have you known Alex?' the man beside her wanted to know.

' Only for a few weeks. He employed me through a mutual friend—my father's solicitor.'

' Did your father write?'

' Textbooks. He died less than a year ago. I miss him very much,' she answered, wondering why she had taken him into her confidence.

' Is that why you came here, to get away from your loneliness?'

' I had to earn a living.'

' But surely—in London,' he protested, ' there must be plenty to do.'

' I suppose I could have got another job,' she conceded, ' but Alex was the first person who came along.'

' Do you always grasp at first chances?'

' Why not? It seemed a wonderful opportunity to see something of the world.' She spread her hands. ' I always thought the Caribbean would be beautiful, but I had no idea how lovely it really is.'

' It can be cruel as well as beautiful,' he warned. ' There is always the reverse side, or so I've discovered.'

She fancied that his mouth had taken on a cynical curve, although she did not turn to look.

' We can all be disappointed,' she acknowledged, ' but I think you love this sea of yours in all her moods.'

' In all her moods,' he agreed, leaving her to stand alone beside the rail.

As the wind freshened the schooner ran before it, wild and free in her natural element. Vanessa supposed she should go below, but there was something about the wind and the sea and the graceful vessel heeling over a little to press herself against the bosom of those dark waves which kept her standing where Max Rossiter had left her. After a while she went for'ard to feel the full force of the wind beating against her, standing at the prow for a long time, like a figurehead with her hair flowing back and her cheeks cool and moist from the fine spray which came up from the bows. The long bowsprit dipped and caught the starlight as it rose again, and the swish of the water running along the hull was like a long-drawn sigh. It seemed to accentuate the silence of the night and this other new feeling of freedom which had entered her heart.

Around midnight Maxwell Rossiter came back to where she stood.

' I thought you would have gone below by now,' he remarked.

' I must have lost count of the time.' She turned with her back to the rail. ' It's easy enough to do that on a night like this.'

He leaned his arms along the rail, looking beyond her, his dark profile silhouetted against the sea. The long line of his jaw and the thin, hawk-like nose made him look every inch the brigand Alex had proclaimed him, yet she was aware of an enormous sense of confidence in him, of the knowledge that he would be a tower of strength in an emergency. Most arrogant men were, she thought. They were sure of what they must do, without hesitation, and so they won the day.

'How long do you intend to stay on the island?' he asked.

'Alex thinks it will take about three months to finish his book.'

'Is it important?'

'The book, or my having to stay at La Sola for three months?'

'I was thinking mainly about the book. He had quite a success with his last one, I understand.'

'And with his latest play. He has one running in London now.'

She could not let Alex's talent go unsung, because she felt an immense pride in her employer's achievements although she had not taken any part in them until now. Alex was so easy to know, so open and above board, while this man—

She paused to consider Max Rossiter once more, but could not read anything in his dark face to encourage her.

'It was his ambition,' he said, 'to write. Alex was always scribbling things on pieces of paper as a boy, but no one really took it seriously. My father thought it a colossal waste of time, in fact. I wonder what he would have said now.'

He was looking down at her, as if he included her in the disturbing fact of his brother's success as a writer.

'Surely you don't resent what he has done,' Vanessa heard herself protesting.

There was a long pause before he answered.

'If you mean am I jealous of Alex's ability to tell a good tale, the answer is no. "Every man to his trade" is an old saying in the Islands, and good luck to him if he enjoys it.'

'You enjoy what you're doing,' she said without hesitation.

'Certainly. Otherwise I wouldn't be doing it.' The slate-grey eyes gleamed under their straight black brows. 'I can't remember when I first learned to sail a boat, but I must have been very young. It's either in your blood or it isn't. Some people are afraid of the sea.

' Is that why you advised me to go below?'

' I don't think you're afraid,' he said.

The steward brought cocoa, hot and black and laced with rum.

' Drink it,' Max advised. ' It will keep out the cold.' He looked up to the wavering mast as the schooner plunged and lurched like a black stallion just held in leash. ' We're making good headway,' he admitted. ' We should be home in record time.'

Vanessa's gaze followed his, watching as a thin ribbon of cloud skimmed between them and the sky. There was something so essentially free about it all, a fascination which she could not quite describe, but she knew that it could so easily ensnare her if she lived here too long. She saw Maxwell Rossiter turn to the wheelhouse as she went below, tall and dark and powerful, a man of the sea, born and bred to it and feeling as much a part of it as she had done.

Remembering Alex, she hurried down the companionway to find his door still firmly closed against intrusion.

' Mister Alex, he go sleep long time,' the steward informed her with a smile. ' I no wake him for hot rum drink.'

Neither should you, Vanessa decided, but she opened her employer's door a fraction of an inch as she passed it to make sure that he was really all right. Alex was lying on his back with his arms flung wide and a most blissful look on his face. It would indeed have been a shame to disturb him.

CHAPTER II

The wind continued to freshen during the night, hurrying them towards their destination. Vanessa slept as soundly as a baby, lulled by the motion of the ship and the hiss of the tide along the thick bulkhead which closed her in. Early in the morning she was awakened by a disc of light wavering on the wall of her cabin, and it was minutes before she realised that it was bright sunlight pouring through the porthole above her head. She lay on her bunk watching the shimmering circle until the native steward came with her morning tea.

'That ol' wind he drop right down, mistress,' he informed her with his engaging grin which seemed to split his dark face in half. 'You see plenty sunshine now!'

The schooner seemed to be motionless now, drifting on the tide.

'Are we there?' she asked in a sort of panic. 'Mr Rossiter said it would be nearer noon before we reached the island.'

'We go slow now, but we make good time all night. Mister Max, he up there in the wheelhouse all night. He sure make her go!' There was frank admiration for their skipper in the sparkling black eyes.

Vanessa drank her tea and was still in her bunk when Alex tapped on her door.

'Lazybones!' he said, opening it. 'Aren't you going to rise and shine?'

There was no sign of his former distress about him now; the sea was calm and his sickness had passed.

'How long before we reach the island?' she asked.

'About an hour, I should think. We've slowed down a little, but Max will get us there just as quickly as he can. He hasn't much time for passengers.'

She was left wondering why Max had put himself out to speak to her the night before out there on the starlit deck.

34

The steward had brought her fresh water in a copper pitcher and she washed her face and hands and tidied her hair. The movement beneath her feet was gentler now and a brilliant sun streamed down from the open hatch as she went in to breakfast. Max was nowhere to be seen, but Alex was consuming eggs and bacon with unbelievable relish.

' I'm famished,' he informed her. ' There's nothing like being under the weather at sea for whipping up an appetite afterwards. Sit down and tuck in. There won't be another meal before we get to La Sola.'

The mention of La Sola made her feel curiously nervous. She had never considered her reception on the island, the reaction she could expect to her presence there, but now, suddenly, it had been thrust upon her by Alex's remark. What would his mother think of her? Would she suspect an affair, not knowing that they had only met a few weeks ago? Maxwell Rossiter had hinted at it when they had first met and no doubt he had discussed the possibility with his mother. Did they expect her to be in love with Alex? Was she already half in love with him?

Certainly she liked him; he had been easy to know and unfailingly kind and she had been impressed by his undoubted success. In spite of his outwardly flamboyant attitude he was genuinely modest, a fact which she found wholly attractive. It was foolish, however, to feel that he might be attracted in return.

By eleven o'clock the wind had died completely and the *Carmelita* drifted southwards with slackened sails, basking in the heat of the strengthening sun. Bequia and Mustique were behind them, dim shapes against the translucent blue, while ahead of them island after island dotted the sea in the long chain of the Windwards. Somewhere along them was their destination.

They came to the island almost too suddenly. It lay on the sea before them, deep green on that incredibly blue water, with curves of dazzling white sand scalloping its shore and a fringe of palms running out to a rocky bluff dominating its northernmost point.

Vanessa thought that she could see a house up there and wondered if it was La Sola.

There were other houses on the beach beneath the bluff, scattered among the palms, and a yacht lying at anchor off shore with its attendant dinghy floating alongside. Other yachts were anchored in the small bay they reached in next to no time, and she wondered if they all belonged to Maxwell Rossiter.

Carmelita came round into the wind and the mainsail was dropped with the precision she had come to expect. Max Rossiter strode along the deck.

' I'll have your luggage sent ashore,' he informed Alex. ' It's been a pleasant enough trip.'

The anchor chain rattled and the schooner turned with her bowsprit to the open sea, as if eager to take off again once they were put safely ashore. They were about three cables' length from the beach and a launch was already coming towards them, streaking through the water to leave a white, curving wake behind it, like churned suds.

' That will be Tom,' Max observed dryly. ' He loves a show of speed.'

The launch circled and came up on the port side, and Vanessa could see the young man at the wheel now and the child sitting beside him. They both had fair hair which had been bleached almost white by the sun and their skin was the colour of rust. The young man waved a greeting while the boy scrambled to the prow of the boat.

As the launch came nearer Vanessa felt a tension in the two men standing beside her. Maxwell Rossiter went forward to the rail.

' Uncle Max! Uncle Max!' the child shouted. ' What have you brought me from Bridgetown?

Alex moved towards the rail to stand beside his brother and Vanessa hung back, leaving the family to meet alone. The child was hoisted aboard and she saw Max turn to make way for Alex, but the little boy flung himself at his uncle, hugging his knees.

' You should have taken me!' he cried. ' I'm big enough now.'

36

Max took him by the shoulders. turning him round to face Alex, and the child held out his hand. It was an almost reluctant gesture, polite and friendly but unloving.

'How do you do?' he said.

Alex put his arm round the boy's shoulders, seemingly at a loss for a moment, and then he turned towards Vanessa.

'This is Robin,' he introduced them. 'Nobody seems to have told him that his father was coming to see him.'

Vanessa looked at him with a sense of shock.

'Your son?' she asked.

'Yes—Robin.' There was a steely glint in his eyes as they held hers.

'I knew you were coming,' the child said.

'But you didn't think I would arrive quite so soon, was that it?' Alex asked.

'We thought you would come with the steamer.' The boy's eager gaze ranged beyond them to the wheelhouse. 'Uncle Max lets me come aboard as soon as he gets in.'

Alex frowned, but only momentarily.

'All right,' he agreed, 'off you go! I suppose your uncle is trying to make a sailor out of you.'

There was resentment there, but if Alex didn't want Max to influence his son why had he left the boy behind at La Sola? Vanessa put the child's age at little more than five years. He looked a strong, healthy little boy with his father's sturdy physique and fair colouring, but in the proud way he tilted his head he could have been Max Rossiter's child. They were a queerly assorted family, she decided, as the tall, leggy youth who had steered the launch across the bay vaulted across the gunwale and stood before her on the deck, waiting to be introduced.

'This is Tom,' Alex said. 'My youngest brother.'

Tom Rossiter held out his hand.

'You must be Vanessa,' he guessed. 'Alex wrote about you. We're all very pleased to have you at La Sola and we hope your stay will be a happy one.'

It was an odd little speech, coming from a seventeen-year-old, but Tom looked older than his years. He was very much like Alex, with fair, straw-coloured hair plastered on his brow and the grey Rossiter eyes which she had come to expect. He was different from Max, certainly, yet he had something of his older brother's intensity as he studied her freely, waiting for her reply.

'What I've seen of the Caribbean has already won me over,' she confessed truthfully enough. 'I've come to work, of course, but I hope I shall be able to play a little, too.' Her eyes slid down to the white launch bobbing beneath them. 'It's all—truly delightful.'

'We'll try to keep you,' he assured her with a smile, 'for as long as we can. Girls are in short supply on the island!'

'You'll get plenty of girls to take up your attention when you go to Cambridge,' Alex said.

Tom frowned.

'I'm not sure that I want to go,' he declared, glancing in Max's direction.

'You'll have no choice if brother Max has a say in it,' Alex returned, 'but you'd be foolish not to go. It's a chance in a million. I think you know that.'

'I suppose I do.' The grey eyes looked resigned. 'All the same, I wish people didn't know what was "best" for other people just because they didn't have the same chance themselves.'

Alex laughed.

'There's logic for you!' he said to Vanessa. 'Would you like to go ashore immediately?' He glanced towards the wheelhouse where Max had taken refuge with his small nephew. 'I think we'll have to leave Robin behind; he practically lives aboard when there's a schooner available, I gather.'

Tom vaulted over the side to help her into the launch. He wore neither socks nor shoes and had his jeans rolled above his knees. His faded cotton shirt was open to the waist and she fancied that he had thrust his arms into it as the launch had approached the schooner after seeing a woman on board.

Max Rossiter stood at the rail to watch them go.

'When will you come ashore?' Tom called up to him. 'Mother's sure to ask.'

'Give me an hour,' Max said. 'I have stores to unload.'

'He could have left that to the crew,' Tom muttered as he bent to start the engine, 'but Max is suspicious of everybody these days. He doesn't believe anyone will do a job properly unless he's around to see to it.'

'Wielding the big whip?' Alex suggested.

'He didn't used to be like that,' Tom answered loyally enough. 'It was only after—'

Suddenly his face flushed scarlet and he lowered his eyes to the engine cowling. There was an embarrassed silence until Alex changed the subject.

'Is Mother all right?' he asked.

'She's been much better these past few days. She likes all the family around,' Tom said, advancing the throttle until the launch streaked away from the schooner's side like a bullet from a gun.

Vanessa's gaze remained focused on the schooner's wheelhouse where she could still see Maxwell Rossiter standing silhouetted against the rigging like the dark-visaged buccaneer he so much resembled. He did not wave nor acknowledge their departure in any way, and she supposed he was glad to be rid of them. Swiftly she turned her head away.

Facing her was a wide semi-circle of beach. It stretched from the rocky bluff she had first seen from the schooner's deck in a broad arc of fine sand to a distant point where a palm grove came down to the water's edge. Many of the trees lay aslant the turquoise-blue sea, steeping their feet in the water while their heads were outlined sharply against the azure sky, but it was the sharp conical shape of the island's only mountain which held her interest longest. It towered above them to the left of the bay and she could see now that the bluff was its natural continuation running down into the sea.

Tom shut off the engine and the launch made straight for the shore, drifting in through the gentle surf to a jetty which stretched a considerable way into the sea. Vanessa understood the reason for its length when she looked over the side. The placid water lapping the jetty steps was transparent and shallow and she could see straight down to the sandy bottom where little coloured fish darted in and out between the piers. Tom promptly jumped over the side, grasping the gunwale to guide them in. He was up to his armpits in blue, translucent water which Vanessa fancied would be warm to the touch.

Alex helped her on to the jetty.

' Welcome to the island,' he said. ' Welcome to La Sola.'

They hadn't reached La Sola yet, and Vanessa was already wondering what Alex's mother would make of her. A woman who ' liked all the family around' might not take too kindly to strangers.

They walked up the beach through a cluster of coconut palms to the dirt road which skirted the bay. There was a row of huts here and a long, shuttered warehouse, which seemed to be out of use. Several Negroes sat in the shade of the hut, whittling sticks or just lounging with their hats over their eyes and their bare toes in the sand. Tom went towards a car parked in the shade of the palms.

' We ought to have a new buggy,' he said, ' but Max just isn't interested in cars. He says there's far more sea around the island than roads on it and buys another boat!'

In spite of his criticism of his piratical brother there was a grudging admiration in his tone.

' If you pass your exams when you get to Cambridge you can buy a car of your own,' Alex pointed out. ' How does Robin behave?'

' Oh, fine. Just fine! He's Max's slave. A willing one, of course,' Tom laughed. ' He would abandon everything to go out with Max, but Mother keeps a firm hand. There are regular lessons and plenty of sleep.' He opened the car door. ' That goes for all of us,' he concluded.

' It doesn't seem to have done you much harm.' Alex glanced at him speculatively. ' Why are you here

40

just now?' he asked. ' I thought you would have been safely tucked away in Bridgetown.'

' It's a holiday,' Tom informed him. ' Something to do with elections and—Mother was ill. Max arranged it,' he added, as if the remark came naturally.

Max runs this place and his family, Vanessa thought. She had yet to meet Helena Rossiter.

Tom drove in his bare feet; he seemed to have left his shoes behind when he had left La Sola that morning, and the soles of his feet were probably as hard as leather.

They went up over the bluff, where there were a few houses scattered among the trees. Most of them were small, with tiny wooden verandahs clinging to their sides, and all of them were half hidden in flowering creepers. Plantains grew in profusion beside each small dwelling and some of them boasted a banana patch, a breadfruit tree and the ubiquitous coco-palm.

' They work at La Sola,' Tom offered by way of explanation, ' but they prefer to live here on this side of the Bluff. They consider it better for the fishing.'

When they finally reached the ridge Vanessa looked back towards the bay where the schooner lay like a painted ship on an emerald sea. There were streaks of peacock blue in the water now, and yellow where it came close to the shore, and far out, beyond the schooner, she could see the edge of the reef where the bluff went down, separating the two bays. It was because of the reef that the schooner had anchored in the larger bay, and it left La Sola isolated.

Turning her face to the smaller bay, she saw a curve of white sand, like a scimitar, stretching the entire length of the lagoon, palm-fringed all the way, with a lace of surf skirting the shore and a distant beach-house lying close under a frowning cliff. The sun, pouring down out of a cloudless sky, lay on the water like a shield and caressed the sugar cane where it stood in the gap between the hills. From the height of the ridge the cane looked like a vast, inland sea stirred into motion by the gentle wind.

Beyond the sugar there were more palms. They looked smaller than the slanted giants overhanging the beach, more uniform, but she had yet to discover the difference.

'We're almost there,' Tom said.

Alex remained silent, and Vanessa wondered what it meant to him to be coming home like this after three years and what had happened to part him from his son for all that time. Surely his wife must be dead when he had not mentioned her. There was a grey look about his face now that they were almost at their destination and his mouth was grim. Some of the essential sorrow of parting had dimmed his habitually-smiling eyes.

La Sola stood half-way down the slope. It was built of stone, with a steep roof which extended over the long verandah running round three sides of it, and a tall hedge of red hibiscus bordered a green lawn backed by a row of tall cequita palms. Beyond it the sugar cane stretched away along the gap for as far as the eye could see.

The main door of the house lay open, as it generally did, to let in as much air as possible. Only when the wind came with rain in its teeth was it closed and the jalousies battened down. Vanessa could hardly imagine that ever happening when she first looked at La Sola and saw how fair it was. Someone, long ago, had planned and planted a garden to look down to the sea, and now it was matured. Massed poinciana and oleander spread colour everywhere and the scent of jasmine drifted strongly towards them as they drew near. It was a fragrance which Vanessa was to associate with her arrival at La Sola for the rest of her life.

Tom brought the car to a standstill. When the engine was shut off there was nothing to be heard but the whispering of the sugar cane as the wind caressed it, a sound that was like a faint sighing, and Vanessa closed her eyes for a moment.

When she opened them to look at the house again a tall woman was coming towards them, leaning heavily on a stick, and, without having to be told, she knew that this was Helena Rossiter.

'Well, Mother,' said Alex. 'How are you?'

'Better than I was, thank goodness.' Piercing grey eyes searched her son's face. 'But of course, I could have been dead for all you knew. You may be able to write books, Alex, but you certainly fall short on your correspondence with your family.'

'I'm sorry,' Alex apologised. 'It was a question of time, but you knew I would come one of these days.'

'Did I?' A thin hand stretched out towards him. 'Well, here you are. Have you seen Robin? He noticed the schooner coming in and was off like a streak of lightning for the bay. Your brothers spoil him.'

Alex drew Vanessa forward.

'I wrote to you about Miss Gilbert. She's going to help with the book,' he explained.

Vanessa faced the older woman's scrutiny as best she could, feeling curiously nervous for no very clear reason. She tried to tell herself that it didn't really matter whether Helena Rossiter liked her or not, but obviously Alex wanted her to be accepted by his family.

'I've told her she'll love La Sola,' he ran on, 'and her help will be invaluable to me.'

Helena offered Vanessa her free hand.

'How do you do?' she said, her keen grey eyes still searching. 'Have you been in the West Indies before, Miss Gilbert?'

'Never,' Vanessa confessed. 'It's all a tremendous adventure for me, a wonderful experience, in fact. I know I'm going to love every minute of it.'

'You came over with the schooner.' Helena was addressing them both now. 'I told Max to look out for you in Bridgetown and save you that dreadful journey on the steamer. Was he at the airport?'

'No,' said Alex. 'I went in search of him, but he wasn't at the Flying Fish, either. Vanessa stumbled across him at the Careenage.'

'I hope he was polite,' Helena said. 'But no

matter! Come away in, Miss Gilbert. I'm sure you'll be glad of a wash and brush up after your unexpected sail.'

She seemed kinder now, more warm. Their first encounter over, she was prepared to put what misgivings she might have had behind her and judge for herself in the future.

La Sola was long and low and rambling. Rooms had been built on to the original structure to accommodate a growing family, giving it an inconsistency which was delightful. The centre of the house was apparently the large, roomy patio with its wrought-iron screen doors leading to a wide, paved area which looked down over a banana plantation to the sea far below. At this distance the Caribbean reflected a dozen shades of green and blue, with a pale yellow band along the horizon marking the distant coral reef. Beyond the reef, from the Lesser Antilles to the Gulf, were the sailing waters which offered Maxwell Rossiter the freedom he had always sought.

Vanessa's bedroom was a sheer delight to her. Like most of the other rooms at La Sola it was open-fronted, with a sliding glass door leading to a small verandah which gave directly on to the garden. There was a table for her convenience and two cane lounging chairs where she could enjoy an uninterrupted view of the lagoon. She would be able to work here very pleasantly in the open, sheltered from the sun by the sloping rattan roof of the verandah with the scent of jasmine floating in from the garden and a little yellow bird hopping about on the blue glazed tiles at her feet.

'You'll find your way around eventually.' Helena Rossiter stood for a moment in the doorway. 'If there's anything else you want just ask. Barbie will look after you. I'll send her along to see to your clothes.'

Vanessa, who had never had a personal maid to attend to her wants, thought that she could do without Barbie, but when the girl arrived, small and shy and smiling, she was captivated. Barbie's lustrous black

44

eyes followed her everywhere, and when Vanessa's suitcases were deposited at the open door she unpacked
them with a childish delight in their content which
made rejection impossible.

'You go shower in Mistress Rossiter's bathroom,'
she suggested eagerly, producing two huge white towels
to match the all-white decor of the room. 'I look
after you both now!'

The bathroom Vanessa was to share with her hostess
was two doors away, a converted bedroom with all the
modern conveniences she could have wished for, and
suddenly she was smiling at her original conception
of life on a Caribbean isle. She had half expected
La Sola to be almost primitive, and here she was
showering in luxury with soft, creamy coco-matting to
walk on all the way back to her lovely room.

Someone had come in with a vase of strelitzia—a
white vase to complement the waxy apricot of the
magnificent blooms—standing it on the little polished
table in the middle of the floor. It gave colour and
life to the room and a suggestion of welcome which she
was quick to appreciate, although it had not been
there when she arrived. Perhaps the mistress of the
house had waited to be sure of her first reactions to
her before she extended the welcoming gesture of
special flowers, or perhaps it was just a Caribbean
custom, one among many which she had still to learn
about.

Paddling across the cool blue tiles in her bare feet,
Vanessa was conscious of a surge of warmth welling in
her. Alex had been kind and his mother was not
resentful of her, apparently. Helena Rossiter had
accepted the fact that her son had work to do and
perhaps she reasoned that he might be persuaded to
stay a little longer in the Caribbean if he could make
his visit a working holiday. Tom had remarked that
his mother 'liked all the family around', and certainly
Vanessa believed that she could work here with a will.

There were distractions, of course. The first came
in the shape of Tom, who appeared on her verandah
with an armful of scarlet hibiscus.

45

' I thought you'd like some,' he announced, dumping the exotic blooms on her dressing-table. ' I expect you will be going to work here, out of the sun, where it's cool,' he added, strolling across the verandah.

' I won't be able to call it work,' Vanessa smiled. ' Sit down, Tom, if you have a minute to spare, and tell me about La Sola.'

' We all have much more than a minute to spare at La Sola, except Max,' he said, stretching out his long limbs on one of the reclining chairs. ' He probably won't come up for a meal for ages yet.'

' Because of me?' She had been quick to detect the implication in his words.

' He doesn't like strangers,' Tom admitted, ' although sometimes he's forced to cope with them. He never takes a charter out himself if there are women aboard.'

' How he must have detested the trip from Barbados!' she said sharply. ' I must remember to keep out of his way.'

' Oh, Max isn't so bad,' Tom conceded. ' It's just that he doesn't like women very much. Not since—'

Again he broke off in mid-sentence, reminding her of his obvious embarrassment as they had come ashore in the launch and he had spoken of Max. The past seemed to trip the Rossiter men up on occasion and Tom was less discreet than his brothers, but once more he had silenced himself just short of an unforgiveable reference to the past. Vaulting to his feet, he stood uncertainly in the middle of the verandah, looking at her almost guiltily.

' What do you think of London?' he demanded, changing the subject. ' I've never been there and I'm not sure that I really want to go.'

' You'll love it,' she assured him. ' And after all, you are going to Cambridge.'

' Does that mean so much?' His level gaze sought the distant sea. ' If Max would have it, I could be useful enough here.'

' But he's decided that you go to England, and England it is,' she suggested.

'You have the situation in a nutshell,' he agreed.

Which meant that Max had the final say in everything connected with La Sola. He had made himself a despot, governing this small kingdom of his with a will of iron, and even his mother came under his sway. Or so it seemed.

'If you've never left the islands, Tom, you ought to go and see something of the world,' she advised. 'I felt that way when I left England. I really hadn't been very far away from home all my life.'

'Have you no family?' His tone was slightly incredulous, as if he could not quite conceive of anyone being alone in the world.

'I have one sister, married in France. She has a very full life. Her husband is a farmer.'

'We were in sugar till Dad died,' Tom mused. 'Then Max decided to branch out. He wanted more than one string to his bow when the sugar prices began to fall, so he turned to his first love and bought up the schooners. Now he has a small fleet of freighters as well, and he runs La Sola as a profitable concern into the bargain. Maybe he has the Midas touch,' he laughed. 'Some people say he has while others aren't so charitable. I know he's hard, but I guess he's also fair.'

There had been no mention of Alex, no suggestion that he had played any significant part in the metamorphosis of La Sola. Somewhere, about the time of his father's death, things had changed for this closely-knit family and Max had taken control. Perhaps that was what he held against Alex, who was the oldest son and who had gone off to follow his own bent when they had needed all the help they could get on the island to save the family fortunes. It was something which could have been forgiven now that La Sola was flourishing, but perhaps Max was the unforgiving kind.

Vanessa thought of him when Tom had gone. His strong personality seemed to dominate the quiet house even in his absence, and she was conscious of an odd tension in her own mind as she waited for his return.

It seemed to matter whether he would like her or not.

Ten minutes later a tray was brought to her room, carried in by Barbie with a great deal of ceremony and placed on the verandah table. It was hot at that hour of the day, although a breeze stirred the creepers to a gentle sighing, and the labourers had left the fields. Vanessa had watched them filing past the house on their way over the Bluff, tall, slouching men with their hands in their pockets and gaily-skirted women carrying baskets on their heads, some of them singing and some laughing; none of them silent for long.

Barbie turned down the white coverlet on the bed behind her.

'You sleep good,' she suggested, folding Vanessa's cotton dressing-gown over a convenient chair. 'One hour, perhaps, then you go see mistress.'

Vanessa knew that she would not be able to sleep in the middle of the day. It was a habit she was yet to acquire, but she realised that Mrs Rossiter probably needed the rest hour.

Isolated in her own room, she could take time to think, to adjust herself to the events of the morning and her arrival at La Sola. She put on the cotton caftan and went out to stand in the shade of the verandah, aware that her view was dominated by the schooner riding at anchor in the adjoining bay. It was far enough out to be seen from the house and she fancied that she could recognise Max moving about on the deck with the diminutive figure of Robin following in his wake. Alex's son, who was Maxwell Rossiter's willing slave!

She sat down at the table to eat the salad Barbie had prepared and found it delicious. After the hearty breakfast she had consumed with Alex on board *Carmelita* she wanted nothing more, but she ate most of the small, fresh pineapple which had been scooped out of its skin, mixed with other exotic juices, and then put back and topped with its crested 'lid'.

After an hour stretched leisurely on one of the cane loungers she crossed to the edge of the verandah, contemplating the wealth of colour and beauty in the garden beneath her. Some of the plants had wilted a little in the heat, but she knew that they would revive immediately when the shade of the house eventually reached them.

There was hardly any sound now. La Sola was asleep, yet she could not imagine either Alex or Tom indulging in the siesta hour. It occurred to her then that Tom might have gone back to the schooner, although she had not heard the car starting up.

And Alex? He could be making his peace with La Sola. If he had not been near the place for three years there would be much for him to catch up on, memories to haunt him, perhaps, old sores to heal. She walked to the edge of the patch of shade which the house was already throwing across the garden, and then she saw him. Alex was standing on the higher ground which rose towards the Bluff, looking down across the ragged banana trees towards the lagoon, and although she could not see his face very clearly he had the look of a man who was trying to come to terms with the past. As he turned away there was no buoyancy in his step and his shoulders were hunched. He was so unlike the Alex she had come to know during these past few weeks that she drew back into the shadow of the house until he had passed.

Then, out of the blue, bedlam broke loose. The sound came from the back of the house and it was as if the silence had been waiting for it. Siesta was over for the day.

Barbie came to collect her tray, humming tunelessly, and the little yellow bird which had haunted the verandah all morning chirped in unison. It darted from pole to pole, in and out of the creepers, sometimes perching almost above Vanessa's head, sometimes flying straight out into the sunlit garden to return and chirp once more.

'You like yellow bird?' Barbie asked conversationally.

'Very much, Barbie, and I did enjoy my lunch—the pineapple,' Vanessa added helpfully.

Barbie's delighted smile spread from ear to ear.

'I bring you pineapple juice to drink,' she offered. 'Plenty pineapple at La Sola!'

Vanessa had visions of endless pineapples cluttering up her room from then on, but she could not disappoint the girl.

'You come take tea with Mistress Rossiter,' Barbie announced. 'I go tell her now.'

'Where?' Vanessa asked, slightly alarmed.

'In she room. I show you.'

Vanessa bathed her face while Barbie waited.

'I suppose I'll get used to the heat in time,' she mused.

'You go take shower,' Barbie suggested, as if that might be the answer to every ill.

'Not again,' Vanessa smiled. 'I can't stand under a shower all day long. It will be cool enough in the evening, I expect.'

Barbie nodded. Obviously she did not understand this preoccupation with coolness.

Vanessa put on a lime green dress and a pair of white sandals. Her fine, silky hair clung in damp little tendrils to the nape of her neck and she brushed it upwards, pinning it high on the crown of her head. Barbie watched, entranced, dark eyes gleaming at her through the mirror.

'It's red,' she said after a moment or two.

'I like to call it auburn,' Vanessa laughed, 'but— yes, perhaps it is just red!'

She walked behind Barbie down the corridor to Helena Rossiter's room.

'Come in!' Helena called through the half open door when she heard their footsteps. 'Tea, Barbie, as quickly as you like!'

She was seated on a deeply-upholstered chaise-longue between the verandah and the bed, with a round, glass-topped table pulled up before her and another chair placed ready for her guest. If she had been asleep it did not show in her eyes. They were brightly alert, taking in all that was going on around her. They were Maxwell Rossiter's eyes.

'Sit down,' she commanded. 'Did you manage to

50

sleep?'

'I find it difficult in the middle of the day.' Vanessa sat on the chair facing her. 'And I slept well enough on the journey from Barbados.'

'You did better than Alex, then.' The perceptive gaze did not leave her face. 'He has never been a good sailor. Is he a successful writer, would you say?'

The unequivocal question embarrassed Vanessa.

'Don't answer if you don't want to,' she was told. 'He must be making a living at it, at least, since he hasn't asked us for help. We look after the boy, and that's all he will let us do.'

'I met Robin when we arrived,' Vanessa said. 'He seemed completely obsesssed by the schooner.'

'It's not so much the schooner as Max,' Helena answered a trifle sharply. 'If Robin had his way he wouldn't learn a thing. He'd be off with Max all the time, roving about the Caribbean, learning to be a pirate.'

She used the word lightly; not as Alex had done.

'Most boys are fond of the sea,' Vanessa said.

'Alex wasn't,' her hostess declared. 'Wild horses wouldn't take him out on one of the piraques when he was a boy, and last night must have been agony for him.' She eased herself in the long chair. 'Help me to my feet,' she commanded. 'It will save me ringing for one of these giggling girls from the kitchen.'

'Ought you to get up?' Vanessa asked, noticing the sparse outline of the older woman's body beneath the loose housecoat she wore.

'Of course I ought to get up! I mean to be sitting in my own chair in the patio when Albert Nagle comes up here from the steamer with his little black box of tricks,' Helena declared. 'His medicines don't do me a ha'pennyworth of good, though he pretends to cure me.' She chuckled, a sound which came from deep in her throat. 'There's no cure for old age, you know, in spite of what Max says. How old are you, Miss Gilbert?'

Vanessa was getting used to abrupt questions.

'I'm twenty-three,' she said.

'Max is twenty-nine.' Helena seemed to compare them. 'High time he married and settled down, but I don't dare tell him so. Not too often, anyway.' She paused before what appeared to be a painful memory. 'Once bitten, twice shy, they say, and maybe that is so, but I'd like to see him with a wife, all the same. He's too much of a loner these days. Time was when he would spend weeks here, on the island, but now it's off to St Lucia and Martinique and Antigua to sail his boats between the Leewards and make a lot of money which we don't really need.'

'Is he a trader?' Vanessa asked, feeling faintly embarrassed by this frank revelation of Max's 'short-comings'.

'No, no, you don't make a lot of money trading between the Islands any more,' Helena assured her. 'Not the sort of money Max likes. He's in the charter-ing business in a big way, ferrying rich Americans from place to place looking for peace. They can't find it in their own country, apparently, and Max knows Hispaniola and the Antilles like the back of his hand. He's sailed the Caribbean since he was a boy. It was his first love and we often thought it was going to be his only one until—' She hesitated in the same way that Tom had done earlier. 'But that's past history and no concern of yours,' she added abruptly. 'You'll like it here at La Sola,' she added. 'We'll make you like it.'

'It won't be hard,' Vanessa told her.

Barbie appeared with the tea tray.

'Alex should be here,' Helena said, looking towards the stable buildings. 'I told him four o'clock and he knows I don't like being kept waiting for my tea, but he has such a poor recollection of time. Maybe that makes him a good writer, but I used to think punc-tuality was a grace. It seems different these days. Alex can go away for years without giving us a thought.'

'Don't sell me short, Mother!' Alex appeared in the open doorway behind them. 'I've been working quite hard all afternoon trying to make something out of the chaos in the library. Where on earth did Max get all those old books? He must have been collecting them for years. Does he ever take time off to read them?'

' Max never takes " time off ", as you call it,' Helena answered, ' but he reads a lot when he's at sea, I gather.' She looked out over the ragged heads of the bananas. 'That child should be up here by now,' she added, ' but he'll be eating salted meat down there in the schooner, I imagine,' she sighed impatiently. ' You'll have to exert a sobering influence on him, Alex, now that you're here. He's been running wild these past two years, aided and abetted by Max.'

Alex frowned, although he did not seem inclined to exert his parental authority where Robin was concerned quite so soon.

' We'll come to that,' he said.

' How long are you going to stay this time?' his mother asked.

' Till my book is ready for the publishers.'

' What does that mean?'

' Two months, maybe three.'

' H'mph! Well, we'll see,' Helena commented. ' Your room is just as you left it,' she added. ' Nothing changed.'

' I noticed,' Alex said abruptly.

' The boy is still in the nursery, of course, although Max thinks he should have graduated to a bedroom of his own by now,' his mother offered.

' I fail to see the point,' Alex said, ' since there's no other occupant for the nursery.'

His tone had been just short of bitter and Helena bit her lip.

' At least, I have a grandson,' she said.

Alex got up to pass the tea cups.

' No one else seems to be putting in an appearance,' he remarked.

Vanessa had hardly expected Max to come after all she had been told about him and she soon forgot about him as Alex put himself out to be a charming companion. In no time at all he was making his mother

53

laugh, chasing the shadows from her eyes and sending a warm colour into her sallow cheeks.

'You were always good for me, Alex,' she declared, laying down her cup and saucer, 'and I find a lot of humour in your books. Oh, yes, I read them,' she added, holding up a restraining hand as he was about to protest. 'Some of them are quite good.'

Alex stole a sidelong glance at Vanessa.

'That should put paid to the old adage about a prophet and his own country,' he remarked dryly. 'I wonder what brother Max thinks, since he appears to be the Oracle around here.'

Helena did not answer him. She had given up looking for Max, apparently, although she still thought that her grandson should have returned by now.

'Let's go and have a look,' Alex suggested, holding out his hand to Vanessa. 'We can walk slowly down to the bay.'

Helena's watchful eyes followed them until they were out of sight. Then she rang for Barbie, commanding her to take the tea things away. Her voice was sharper than usual.

Alex and Vanessa heard the summoning bell as they walked down through the banana plantation.

'Mother seems to think I've fallen down in my attempt to bring up Robin as a true Rossiter,' Alex reflected, 'but I thought it was better to leave him here at La Sola. I don't agree with the idea of a child being dragged around the world at his parents' heels; not a child like Robin. I knew he would have a happier life on the island and I made my decision quite deliberately.'

'You—felt that you had to get away?' Vanessa found herself asking, although the last thing she wanted to do was to pry into his private affairs.

'Yes.' The monosyllable was the abruptest thing she had ever heard and it effectively silenced her. Alex had no intention of discussing the past with her or anyone else, it seemed. 'I've more or less cleared the library,' he informed her, 'so we can work in peace

54

there.'

'What about your brother? Doesn't he use the library?'

'He may do when he's here,' Alex conceded, 'but as far as I can gather, he seldom is. He does accounts, of course, but he has a den in another part of the house. We can but wait and see,' he added. 'If Max objects, we'll have to go. The library was my father's domain. It was a sort of business-room-cum-reading-room where we were all welcome. Perhaps that was why he was never able to concentrate on making La Sola pay.'

More and more he was bringing out the hardness in Max, holding his brother responsible, perhaps, for what had happened between them, and Maxwell Rossiter wouldn't deign to defend himself.

Walking closely behind him along the narrow pathway between the banana trees, she felt that Alex had returned to La Sola for a purpose, but what that purpose was she could not imagine. He took her hand to help her down on to the beach, keeping it firmly in his as they walked towards the Bluff.

When the tide was out it was possible to climb over the low ridge of rock which separated the two bays, and even from here she could see the schooner anchored ahead of them, riding gently on the blue water, like a bird. There was very little sign of activity aboard as far as she could see.

'They must be on their way back to La Sola,' Alex said, but Vanessa felt that Max was still aboard *Carmelita*, watching them, perhaps, as they strolled along the beach, resenting them. She slipped her hand from her employer's grasp.

Alex lapsed into silence and she allowed herself to revel in the warm caress of the sun. It was almost impossible to believe that it was February and England was in the grip of winter, with a bitter wind blowing and snow on the hills, perhaps. Here, too, a wind blew against her cheek, but it was the soft trade wind that seamen loved. She thought of how eagerly she had turned her face to it the evening before and of how Maxwell Rossiter had looked at her, as if he found it hard to believe that she could love the sea.

Alex guided her towards the dust road where the tall palms lay aslant the beach.

'Come and see all we have to offer in the way of a village,' he invited. 'It isn't far.'

'Shouldn't we be getting back?'

'Not for another hour, at least,' he said. 'We've got time and to spare.'

There seemed to be no one in sight at first, but gradually, as they walked along, Vanessa became aware of slight, shadowy figures lurking behind the palms. Faces appeared from nowhere to watch, smile and disappear as silently. One minute a colourful skirt could be seen behind a tree; the next it had gone.

'They're shy, but incurably inquisitive,' Alex said. 'They'll know all about you by now.'

'I wonder if I've passed muster.'

'Why not?' He felt for her hand again. 'You're attractive enough, heaven knows!'

Vanessa laughed.

'It's as if you regretted the fact!'

'Why should I?' His look was almost possessive. 'I realise you could have been the perfect secretary and a Gorgon to boot!'

'Don't flatter me too much!'

They had come to the village, which was little more than a cluster of huts, a schoolhouse under a tree, and a wooden church with a square belfry where the bell hung crookedly. A group of natives, their work in the cane fields over for the day, had gathered in front of the store, arguing among themselves about nothing. When Alex approached they touched their battered headgear, glancing at Vanessa at the same time with wide, toothy grins.

Vanessa's attention was focused elsewhere, however. Further up the street a man and a little boy were about to embark on a journey. Maxwell Rossiter had seated his small nephew on a donkey and was leading his own horse towards the Bluff.

'What goes on?' Alex's brows drew together in a

swift frown. 'He's too young for that, wouldn't you say?'

'Donkeys are easy to ride,' Vanessa said. 'They seem to understand children.'

'Why didn't Max ask my permission first?' Her companion's face was now a dull red. 'After all, I am Robin's father.'

'Robin could have had the donkey for some time.'

She was sorry as soon as she had made the observation because it had sounded like an accusation. If you had been here, she had said, in effect, you would have known about the donkey, you would have had the right to object, but as it is, your son has had to rely on Max for guidance and everything else.

'We'll soon see,' Alex said, walking faster. 'It doesn't look as if he can ride properly.'

Robin saw them from his vantage point on the donkey's back.

'Look what I've got!' he yelled. 'A real live donkey. She's called Rosalind. Uncle Max bought her from one of the Indians.'

Max had halted at their approach, his direct gaze challenging his brother as they met.

'I'd have waited,' Alex said. 'Some of these beasts are most unreliable.'

'I checked on this one.' Max acknowledged Vanessa with the briefest of nods. 'She has a character worthy of a thoroughbred and I thought it was time Robin learned to ride.'

'*You* thought?' For a moment Alex looked ugly. 'All right, I suppose I bought that one, Max, but in future I'll make the decisions, if you don't mind.'

Max shrugged.

'So you should,' he returned. 'You're his father.'

Alex grasped the donkey's leading-rein.

'You needn't remind me,' he said. 'I'm perfectly well aware of the fact.'

The tension between them was like a taut cord, ready to snap at any moment, but suddenly Max relieved it by turning his horse's head towards the Bluff and riding off in the direction of La Sola.

For a moment Robin looked disappointed, but pride in his new possession soon consoled him.

'Uncle Max promised it to me for my birthday,' he explained, fondling Rosalind's ears. 'Isn't it the most beautiful donkey you've ever seen?'

He had drawn up just short of calling Alex 'Daddy', and Vanessa wondered if Alex noticed, but he seemed to be preoccupied by the safety factor of his son's new acquisition, checking rein and stirrups as he led the little animal along in the grey dust of the road.

Robin chattered most of the way, a bright spot of excitement appearing on both cheeks as they went up over the Bluff. Rosalind picked her way with the greatest of care, proving to them how right Max had been in his choice.

'I have to feed her and keep her nicely brushed,' Robin explained, 'and then she'll be very fond of me.'

'I'm sure!' Alex said, smiling up at him as he placed a friendly hand on his bare knee. 'Kindness is the greatest thing, old son. We ought to practise it more.'

And forgiveness, Vanessa thought, although it seemed that the brothers were very far away from forgiving each other.

Max had not yet reached La Sola when they arrived, but they saw him riding in half an hour later when Alex and Robin had bedded Rosalind down for the night. Perhaps he had deliberately given them time to do the job together, or perhaps he had just been checking on the work that had been done in the fields in his absence. It was difficult to decide which.

CHAPTER III

When the doctor came to La Sola the following afternoon he was met by the mistress of the house in person. Helena had dressed up for the occasion, putting on her most flattering cotton gown, and there was a bright spot of defiant colour in each cheek as she faced him.

' I have my family home,' she announced, as if that alone might be a cure for her ailment, and the little man nodded, putting away his stethoscope.

' Yes, indeed!' said he. ' I saw Alex as I came up and he tells me he's to write his next book here. Does it mean that—'

' No.' The flush deepened in his patient's cheeks. ' And now you must stay to tea,' she said, ' and to dinner, too, if you have a mind. After that, you can go to see Mrs Camp. She's well enough. I had a word with her the day before yesterday.'

' When did your guests arrive?' he asked, sitting down in the chair opposite her.

' Max brought Alex and his secretary over on the schooner.' There was emphasis in the fact. ' He met them at Bridgetown.'

' A young lady?' Albert Nagle asked.

' A very nice girl. Young, yes, but efficient, I would say.'

If Vanessa had heard them she would have smiled. She was prepared to believe that Helena would take her own time to sum her up and, once or twice, as they had sat over their meal the evening before, she had caught her hostess looking down the length of the table at her with a puzzled frown between her eyes. Helena was still very much the head of the family, sitting in the tall, carved chair at the top of the table while Max sat at the foot. There had been no suggestion that Alex should usurp Max's place, even though he was the oldest son. He had forfeited that right some time ago.

The meal had been pleasant enough, all five courses

of it, eaten by candlelight, with giant moths flying in from the garden to hover above the flames and the disturbed twitter of birds in the hibiscus outside. A great golden moon had risen over the bay, working its way across the cloudless sky above the palms and sending long, dark shadows among the rustling banana fronds. It had been a night of magic overlaid with the odd tension which she had felt from the beginning, but it had ended in laughter as Tom had demonstrated Limbo for Vanessa none too successfully. He had ended up on his hands and knees, creeping under the fire bar at a safe height of two feet, and a series of suppressed giggles emanating from the kitchens had assured them that they were being watched by the experts.

Rising early in the morning, Vanessa had gone in search of Alex, wondering if he was ready to begin work.

'Good gracious!' he had protested, 'I'm not a slave-driver. I mean to show you the island before we put our noses to the grindstone.'

Vanessa gathered that there was plenty of time for everything at La Sola. During the morning she had helped Alex to organise the library into a working unit. Tom had gone off to fish, taking Robin with him, but there had been no sign of Max since he had wished them good-night in the small hours of the morning after watching his brother's unsuccessful attempt at Limbo dancing. Tom had said, vaguely, that he would be 'somewhere around' and Vanessa felt that he, at least, would be working.

Her midday meal was brought to her on a tray again, but this time Alex joined her on her verandah.

'How are you settling in?' he wanted to know. 'Are you comfortable?'

She glanced beyond him to her cool, white and blue bedroom.

'I can't think of anything more I could possibly wish for,' she told him. 'Your mother is being extremely kind.'

'Because she likes you.' His eyes travelled over

her, taking in her gleaming hair and the cool linen dress and her slim bare legs stretched out under the table. 'She'll take her time about admitting it, though, and she might possibly be influenced by Max, but in the end, I think you'll win.'

'It sounds like a battle between Max and me.' She tried to smile. 'Why does he object to women so much?'

Alex poured their fruit juice.

'Who told you that?' he asked quietly.

'I—it's the general impression I gathered.'

'Maybe he does.' He set the jug back on the tray and sat gazing at it for a minute or two. 'I'll admit he's changed,' he said, 'but give the devil his due, he's taken on most of my responsibilities here at La Sola.'

'Does that mean you might be thinking of staying for good?'

He got up from his chair to pace to the edge of the verandah, where he stood looking out across the banana field to the sea.

'I wonder if I could,' he said, 'but I don't think so. Wanderlust is in my blood and every so often I get itchy feet and I have to go.'

'Yet you did think of settling down once before?'

'Yes,' he said, but that was all.

When Barbie came to remove the tray he followed her out.

'I suppose I'd better stay around and have a word with Doctor Nagle,' he decided. 'Will you rest?'

'I tried to yesterday and found it impossible. Too many new impressions,' Vanessa confessed. 'Perhaps I could go for a short walk.'

'Take a hat, if you do,' he advised. 'Certainly you'll have the bay to yourself.'

'I won't go far.' She hesitated. 'I really am dying to plunge myself into that lovely green water. Is it safe to bathe anywhere inside the reef?'

'Practically anywhere. Are you a good swimmer?'

'Fair. Maybe I'll meet Tom and Robin,' she added, smiling up at him.

Alex looked pleased.

' Robin could do with a younger woman's influence,' he said. ' Mother tries, but I think it's a strain on her.'

He went off in search of Helena and Vanessa took up the book she had meant to read, but very soon she was restless. There was so much to see, so many places yet to explore.

Tying a headscarf under her chin, she took her bathing suit and a towel and went down through the banana grove towards the beach. The sun beat down on her, but she revelled in its warmth, turning her face up to it as she walked. The world about her was steeped in a blissful silence; there was no sound anywhere because there was no wind. Even the gentle trades were asleep in this green and golden world where the long bluff stretched out into an emerald lagoon and there was not a cloud visible on the serene and placid horizon.

Walking barefoot on the fine white sand, she allowed time to drift away from her, thinking and not thinking. Far out beyond the lagoon the sun caught the hull of a tiny boat and she supposed it was Tom and Robin fishing near the reef.

When she thought about the child she automatically thought of Alex—and Max. They both loved Robin; perhaps they both wanted him. Certainly Alex had been resentful of his brother's dominance where the boy was concerned.

When she had climbed over the Bluff she could see the schooner again, with another, smaller ship lying alongside. It was probably the freighter which had come in on the morning tide, bringing the doctor and their quota of stores and other necessities from Barbados. A fussy little tender plied between ship and shore, but there was no sign of life on the schooner.

Vanessa remembered their journey from Bridgetown as she walked along the silvery sand. This time she walked close to the sea, letting the little waves drift over her feet, an experience she remembered from childhood, although the stinging chill of the North Sea was a world removed from the caress of the emerald Caribbean.

Choosing a cleft of the rocks for cover, she changed into her swimsuit, leaving her sandals and cotton dress to look after themselves as she plunged straight into the calm green water beneath her.

Immediately she became aware of a strong undertow, but she was not in deep water and she eventually made her way back to the beach. In the shallows she could swim with impunity, and she struck out across the bay, floating on her back after a while to look up into the brilliant blue of the afternoon sky. Idly she turned over, swam a little way, and floated again. This was heavenly! Perhaps she was drifting too near to the Bluff again, but she could swim away as soon as she felt the danger. The sun seemed to be striking straight down into her body, warming her as she lay there, almost lulling her to sleep.

The other swimmer had reached her even before she realised she was not in undisputed possession of the bay. It was Max, and he was angry. He threshed through the water towards her with a rapid, overarm stroke which brought him to her side before she could turn to face him.

' You've no right to be here,' he informed her brusquely. ' Surely you were warned?'

' To keep away?' She swept the hair out of her eyes to frown at him. ' I didn't know this side of the Bluff was your private preserve, Max, otherwise I would have avoided it.'

He ignored her remark.

' Even though you can swim quite well,' he said, ' the Bluff is dangerous. There's a strong undertow. On a rough day it can be lethal.'

' I felt it,' she was forced to admit. ' But I could have pulled away from it again.'

' Don't be too sure.' His tone was ominous. ' On an outgoing tide you wouldn't have a chance, so don't be misled. The Caribbean can be as treacherous as anywhere else.'

She shaded her eyes, blinking the water out of them.

63

'Did you come all the way over from the schooner to tell me that,' she demanded, 'or was it just to warn me off in a general way?'

'I enjoy a swim at this time of the day,' he informed her, 'but that's no reason why you shouldn't share the bay. It's big enough for both of us, I suppose.'

Now that he had offered his warning about the Bluff he looked indifferent.

'But you would rather I kept to the lagoon,' she suggested, treading water furiously.

'One way or the other, I'm not particularly involved,' he answered. 'I thought it was my duty to warn you about the Bluff if Alex hadn't.'

'Thank you,' she said, feeling that she had been slightly foolish. 'I'll remember in future. It was such a glorious day that I couldn't resist a swim. I don't suppose Alex dreamed that I would come this far. He probably expected me to keep to the lagoon. I may do that in future.'

He smiled at the reserve behind the last remark.

'There's no need,' he assured her, 'provided you avoid the Bluff. Really, the water is far more pleasant further along the beach.'

They swam towards the shore, the water lapping gently under their chins.

'This is wonderful!' Vanessa exclaimed. 'I could stay here all day long.'

'Has Alex given you a holiday?'

Something in his tone made her angry again.

'He isn't ready to begin work yet, but we did manage to tidy up the library this morning. Alex is going to use it.'

'Provided I don't mind? That's thoughtful of him. You're welcome to the library,' he added briefly. 'When I'm at La Sola I can find somewhere else to work.'

'I—we understood you weren't there very often.'

He laughed briefly.

'Was that Alex's only reason for taking possession, I wonder?'

'He probably considered that it was the most available room, out of everyone's way,' Vanessa defended her employer.

'Was that what he thought?' Max turned his dark head to look back at her, the water gleaming on his hair. 'Did you come here hoping to marry him?'

She opened her mouth to protest, but a gulp of water choked the words back in her throat.

'Don't lose your calm,' he advised maddeningly. 'It was a perfectly natural assumption on my part.'

'I told you why I came,' she spluttered. 'I had no other reason, but I suppose you had to think the worst of me.'

He braced himself for the long swim back to the schooner.

'My dear Vanessa,' he said carelessly, 'I don't even think of you at all. I saw you were in danger and I swam over to warn you about the currents, that was all. I hope you will be warned. We had an emergency when Robin's mother wouldn't listen to reason and I don't want to contend with another one.'

Anger rose up, threatening to choke her again.

'You don't have to feel responsible for me!' she flashed.

'I wasn't responsible for Robin's mother,' he said harshly, 'but I happened to be there at the time. She panicked and almost lost her life.'

It was the first time anyone had mentioned Alex's wife, and he had not named her, which was strange. Twice he had referred to her as 'Robin's mother', but that was all. They were a strange family in many ways, Vanessa thought, watching as Maxwell Rossiter swam away from her towards the schooner anchored in the bay.

Reaching the shore, she sat in the shallow water, feeling it warm and comforting against her skin while the sun shone down on her back, drying it in less than no time. She was here to work, as she had just told Max, but this was a bonus she was perfectly willing to accept.

Tom came in search of her, his fishing trip over. He had been swimming near the forbidden Bluff.

' I saw you talking to Big Brother,' he remarked as she waded towards him through the surf. ' What do you think of him?'

' Max? I've only known him for a few hours,' she protested. ' I couldn't possibly answer your question, Tom.'

Although it seemed that she had known Max for a very long time, she could not say so to this impulsive younger brother of his who might repeat her confession without intending to hurt.

' Which means you'll reserve your opinion of him for a later day,' Tom suggested. ' It might be the wisest thing to do.'

' Have you decided about Cambridge yet?' she asked, in an attempt to turn the conversation away from his brother.

' I don't know whether I've got a choice or not,' Tom returned gloomily. ' As things stand, I fear Max is going to insist, and one does as he says around these parts.' He flung himself face down on the soft white sand, leaning on his elbows. ' I suppose it's only fair,' he concluded. ' Max has played father for so long now.'

' Your mother would like to see him married,' Vanessa mused, looking out across the bay.

' " To some nice girl "! Yeah, I know, but my guess is that Max will never marry. Not after Diane. She was his one and only love, I suspect, and I guess he never forgave her.'

' Because she married someone else?'

Tom looked startled.

' Didn't you know?' he asked. ' She married Alex.'

Vanessa could not hide her shocked surprise. This, then, was the real conflict between the brothers— Alex's wife, together with the fact that Alex had deserted La Sola. But where was Diane now? Dead, perhaps, since her child was living on the island in the care of his grandmother. Nobody spoke about Diane, and certainly Alex had never mentioned his marriage until Robin had come aboard the schooner, shouting his greetings to Max.

'Don't look too surprised,' Tom admonished. 'We never talk about Diane, as a rule. We may not be much of a family, but we do stick together in a crisis.' He got to his feet, stretching in the sun. 'How do you feel about another swim?' he asked. 'I'll race you across the bay!'

'You'd beat me to a frazzle!' she laughed, getting up to stand beside him. 'Have we time?'

'All the time in the world!'

He laughed down at her, his eyes so like Alex's that it could have been his brother standing there digging his toes into the sand. Only Max was different, she thought, dark and unfathomable, with his emotions shut tightly away behind those steel-grey eyes of his and no clemency in his heart.

'You'll have to play fair and give me a start,' she called over her shoulder as she ran ahead of Tom down the beach, 'and I suppose you'll win, anyway.'

'I'll do my best,' he assured her with a grin. 'Where to? D'you think you could manage the schooner?'

'No!' she protested. 'Not the schooner!'

'Afraid of Max, are you?' he laughed, already level with her. 'Where, then? I'll race you to the dinghy. It's moored out there beside the launch.'

She saw the slim little sailing dinghy lying just short of the schooner, but it was neutral ground and by this time Maxwell Rossiter would be back at work.

'I'll give you a two-minute start,' Tom offered.

The water was so gloriously warm that she plunged into it with a sense of delight, striking through the gentle foam of surf to the blue-green depths beyond. She could see straight down to the bottom, to the clear white sand and the coloured shells and the tiny fish darting away from her shadow as it passed between them and the light. Under the surface something dark floated towards her and she veered away from it, knowing a moment of panic, but it was only a submerged banana leaf torn from its parent tree during a tropical storm.

Where the bay deepened she could see the edge of the coral reef stretching out from the Bluff and instinctively she swam away from it. Max's warning was still very clear in her mind.

The schooner was directly ahead of her now, with the tender at her stern, but there was no longer any sign of activity aboard either vessel. The schooner's gracious lines were silhouetted sharply against the pale blue of the horizon, but she seemed to be deserted. Nearer at hand, the bright red dinghy bobbed on the tide, sharing a buoy with the launch which Tom had brought to meet them the day before.

'You're flagging!' Tom was less than a yard behind her. 'You'll have to go fast to beat me now!'

She acknowledged the boyish challenge with a toss of her head, renewing her effort to reach the dinghy before him, but he passed her easily, swinging himself up into the rocking little craft to wait for her.

'We use it as a raft,' he explained as he helped her on board, 'when it's not in action. It really belongs to Max.'

What doesn't? The thought flashed through Vanessa's mind as she squeezed the sea water out of her hair.

'Max would find us something to eat if we went as far as the *Carmelita*,' Tom suggested. 'Think you could make it, after all?'

'I'd rather not.' She could see the schooner out of the corner of her eye and there seemed to be a movement on deck, as if they had been observed.

'Just as you say.' Tom stretched out on the sun-blanched deck. 'But the *Carmelita* would be much more comfortable.'

'All the same, I'd rather not go any farther.' She hoped she had sounded decisive enough.

'What's the matter?' Tom demanded. 'Has brother Max scared you off? I saw him talking to you over there beside the Bluff.' He rolled over on his side to look at her. 'I wouldn't worry about it if he has,' he added. 'I expect it's only because of Alex—because you're his girl. Old Max isn't really an ogre.'

Vanessa tossed her hair back from her face.

'Tom, I'm not "Alex's girl", whichever way you

68

mean that,' she said firmly. 'I'm his secretary. I'm here to type the manuscript of his new book; nothing more.'

Tom smiled up at her.

'I'll remember,' he promised readily enough, 'but Alex has a way of involving people. When he said he was bringing you out here, my mother wondered—'

He left the sentence unfinished in the tantalising way he had when he wasn't sure of what he had been about to say, but, since she was involved, Vanessa asked another question.

'What happened to Diane? Don't tell me if you don't want to,' she added hurriedly.

He shrugged.

'Nobody quite knows what became of her,' he admitted. 'Not even Alex, I suspect. She decided La Sola was not for her shortly after Robin was born, but when she went off to Barbados, en route for New York, and wanted to take Robin with her, Alex put his foot down. He was backed by my mother, of course, and Robin was really far too young to go chasing round the world with Diane. She believed that she was a good actress and felt that she was being cheated leading the life we do here. Alex thought it was all a flash in the pan at first, but when he finally went after her she just seemed to have melted into thin air. Nobody knew where she was and she appeared to be content with the arrangements we had made for Robin at La Sola.'

'Did Alex come back to the island?'

Tom shook his head.

'He may have gone in search of Diane—further afield. We don't really know. I was fairly young at the time,' he added, 'but I'd learned not to ask too many questions. It was a dark period at La Sola. Max took charge and we did as he said. He seemed obsessed with the thought of Diane, wanting her back on the island, possibly for Robin's sake, but he *had* been in love with her, too. Alex's marriage didn't last very long.'

'Were they divorced?'

Tom shook his head.

'I shouldn't think so. Alex rarely mentioned Diane in his letters home and neither did we when we wrote to him, but—somehow I thought he might have told you.'

He was looking at her searchingly, confused by the situation in spite of his assumed maturity.

'There was no reason why he should,' Vanessa returned almost sharply. 'Ours is a purely business relationship.'

'You could come to care for him,' he pointed out in the blunt way he had which reminded her of Max. 'I think Mother would like that.'

'You're talking nonsense!'

'Why are you blushing, then?'

She covered her face with her hands.

'I'm not! Blushing has gone out of fashion. Didn't you know? I'm just—very warm.'

'I'll take your word for it,' Tom laughed. 'Want to swim again?'

'No.' She could see Max at the rail of the *Carmelita*. 'I've done enough for one day.'

Her swimsuit had dried in the sun. It was a bright tomato-red with a flash down one side, and it was probably most conspicuous. There could be no doubt at all that it would be seen from the deck of the schooner. She dived into the water after Tom as he struck out for the beach.

'Where did you leave your towel?' Tom asked as they ploughed their way through the surf.

'Over by the Bluff. It's a fair way to walk if you want to come back to the schooner.

Tom shrugged.

'Not me,' he declared. 'Max would find me a job to do.'

When they had collected her beach-dress and the towel they climbed back over the Bluff, Tom still barefooted, although Vanessa had buckled on her sandals.

'You'll get to be like a mountain goat if you live here long enough,' he assured her. 'We all went bare foot when we were kids. There's something free about it—getting close to the soil. I'm going to miss all this when I'm packed off to Cambridge.'

'There will be other compensations. I should be back in London by then, so—'

'If I need a guide or mentor, you could oblige?'

'It was just an idea.'

'Alex may want to stay here longer than that.'

'Even so, he'll finish his novel and my work will be finished, too.'

He pondered her remark until they reached the house. The doctor was just leaving.

'I've told your mother she must rest,' he said, shaking hands with the youngest member of Helena's family, whom he had brought into the world seventeen years before. 'So you must all see that she does so.' He looked across at Vanessa. 'I'm glad she has someone of her own sex to talk with,' he smiled. 'It makes a difference when she's had to grapple with a house full of men all her life.'

'You'd think I wasn't capable of running my own life,' Helena commented from her chair on the verandah. 'Where have you been?' She looked directly at Vanessa.

'We went for a swim,' Tom explained. 'Did Robbie bring the fish home?'

'Some of it,' Helena smiled. 'I've a fair notion that we'll find a trail of dead fish all the way back to the shore. Alex has already salvaged about six.'

'What a waste of effort!' Tom grinned. 'There was more than a dozen when he set off from the beach.'

'You'll have to string them next time,' the doctor advised. 'They slip out of a bucket!'

'All the same, you'll be having them for dinner if you'll stay,' Helena said. 'Please do. I'll send word to Mrs Camp and Max or Alex will drive you over later on.'

They were old friends and the doctor's visits were an occasion at La Sola. Soon there was great activity in the kitchens, with much giggling as the fish were prepared for the table. Alex and the doctor strolled out towards the plantation, while Tom helped his mother into the house.

'Can I do anything?' Vanessa asked.

'You can ring for Barbie and tell her I need her,' Helena said. 'When we have a guest for dinner everybody congregates in the kitchen.'

'If you would let me do your hair,' Vanessa suggested, 'I'd love to help.'

Helena paused to look at her.

'Why not?' she agreed. 'It would be taking Dr Nagle's advice!'

Robin came running along the verandah in their wake.

'Where's Uncle Max?' he demanded.

'On the schooner,' Tom informed him.

'No, he's not. He came up with Mr Bradley. I want Mr Bradley to see my donkey—Rosalind.'

His grandmother raised her eyebrows.

'Isn't it time you were thinking about bed?' she enquired.

Robin's face fell.

'It's not dark yet,' he protested.

'It soon will be.' Helena ruffled the fair, bleached hair. 'On you go and show Mr Bradley your donkey,' she said indulgently.

Robin directed his gaze towards Vanessa.

'Would *you* like to see Rosalind again?' he asked shyly.

'Perhaps to-morrow,' Vanessa promised. 'Rosalind may not like too many people visiting her at once. It might upset her just before she goes to bed.'

Robin nodded in agreement.

'I get upset when too many people see me before I go to sleep,' he remarked sagely.

'You mean you bawl your head off when they go away!' Tom teased. 'You get frightened in the dark!'

'Tom!' his mother admonished. 'That will do.'

'I'm not frightened,' Robin protested stoutly. 'I'm going to be a pirate, like Uncle Max!'

'Whatever gave you that idea?' Tom grinned.

'People are much too free with their remarks around

these parts,' Helena said angrily as Robin ran off in search of his uncle. 'I've a fair idea where Robin picked up that one,' she added. 'Max ought to get rid of the Milford man. He's a traitor.'

'Max relies on him,' Tom answered, 'and he's a good skipper. About the best there is in the whole of Hispaniola, I would say.'

'Being able to steer a ship around the Caribbean doesn't automatically make a man trustworthy,' Helena retorted. 'But Max won't be warned.'

The conversation lingered in Vanessa's mind as she helped Mrs Rossiter to dress. Helena had great difficulty in lifting her arms above her head these days and she was still a proud woman. Her hair, which had always been her crowning glory, was difficult to arrange under such a handicap and she watched Vanessa through the mirror with an appreciative smile on her lips.

'You must think me a vain old woman,' she said, 'but I have always been particular about my hair. Barbie arranges it well enough, but she loses interest when it comes to brushing.' She sighed. 'I had half a mind to cut it off a few weeks ago, it got so untidy.'

Her long, silken hair was only lightly flecked with grey, a few fine silver threads mingled with the copper-gold which must have shone in the sun when she was a girl. Her head was set proudly on a long, slender neck and she had good shoulders, but the rest of her body was painfully thin.

'You'll rest for a while?' Vanessa asked when her task was complete.

'And spoil my lovely hair-do!' Helena protested. 'No, I'll sit here in the chair with my feet up till Max comes. That will please him,' she added. 'He likes to see me doing as I'm told.'

'So you should!'

Max was standing in the doorway behind them. How long he had been there was difficult to say, but he had probably seen Vanessa putting the finishing touches to his mother's hair. She stood back, half shyly, as he came into the room.

'How do you like my pretty hair-do?' Helena demanded. 'Vanessa is very clever at it.'

Max gave Vanessa a long, penetrating look.

'Vanessa is clever at a good many things, apparently,' he said abruptly, 'but can you really lie down with all that on top of your head?'

'Don't be silly!' Helena admonished. 'It's my own hair and I don't mean to spoil Vanessa's handiwork by going to bed before dinner. I'll do as you say, though, and rest here on the chaise-longue. I have a book to read.'

'Which reminds me,' Max said, 'about the library.' He looked deliberately at Vanessa. 'I understand you mean to use it to type my brother's manuscript.'

'I didn't insist.' Vanessa wondered why he hadn't approached Alex. 'I could just as easily work on my verandah. It's so cool and fresh out there.'

'We have rain at times, even in the Caribbean,' he pointed out, 'which would mean you would have to work in your bedroom. There's no need for that. I can move out of the library if you can give me a day to collect my things.'

She felt at a disadvantage, depriving him of the room he had used for so long as an office, but surely he need not have involved her. It had been Alex's decision, which she had gone along with as a matter of course, but perhaps it was the arbitrary way in which Alex had taken possession of the library which had irked him.

'Can I help you to move your papers?' she asked diffidently.

'I'll manage,' he said, but Helena was quick to intervene.

'Why not, Max? Vanessa tells me that Alex won't be ready for her for a day or two. He has a lot of revision to do.'

Max hesitated.

'There isn't much,' he said, 'but I have two charters going out at the week-end, so I shall be pretty busy.'

'Then please let me help in the library,' Vanessa begged, feeling that she owed him something. 'If you

74

tell me what to do I can get a start in the morning.'

'What about your swimming adventures?' he demanded. 'The morning is the best time for the lagoon.'

Which meant 'keep out of the bay', Vanessa thought.

'Perhaps I can find time for both,' she suggested. 'I really ought to be working.'

'Since Alex employs you, hadn't you better ask him?' he said.

'I don't think he'll object, but I will ask.'

He followed her as she moved to the door.

'I'll be off early in the morning,' he informed her, 'I'll show you where to put my things.'

Helena watched them go with an odd little smile on her lips.

'You can get someone to help you carry the books,' Max told Vanessa as he marched through the quiet house ahead of her, leading the way to his new 'office'. 'Barbie will tell one of the boys. There are plenty of them around, goodness knows.'

The room which Tom had described to her as Max's 'den' was at the back of the house looking out over the sugar plantation to the hills. It was situated at the end of a long, bare corridor and had probably been some sort of store room at one time where things could be delivered through the garden without going into the house and it probably suited Max very well, since he could come and go as he liked without having to pass through the living rooms.

'Here we are,' he said, indicating the sparsely-furnished interior. 'You can pile everything on the desk or on the floor. I'll arrange the books when I can.'

The room could have been made more attractive, Vanessa thought, but it apparently suited him as it was.

'I meant to move in here a while ago,' he confessed. 'The view from the window is good for me. It reminds me that we started in sugar.'

'You prefer the sea, though. Alex said you were always fond of it.'

He frowned at her reference to his brother.

'Alex wouldn't understand that,' he said brusquely. 'He didn't understand sugar, either.'

She flushed at the reference to her employer's defection.

'Sometimes a man has to follow his own particular star, Mr Rossiter.'

'Max, surely? I've decided to call you Vanessa, since you are apparently here to stay.'

'For three months.' She emphasised the fact deliberately. 'Until Alex's book is finished.'

'You're knowledgeable about that sort of thing?'

'I took a course in typing and bookkeeping, and I can spell!'

A brief smile touched his lips.

'If I don't see you before I leave in the morning,' he said, 'I'd better say " thanks " now.'

'You don't have to thank me,' she told him. 'It's something I think Alex would want me to do.'

'You must be a first-class secretary.' He continued to study her. 'Does my brother appreciate the fact?'

'I haven't asked him.' She was standing at the window now, looking out across the murmuring cane. 'I've never seen sugar growing before,' she reflected. 'I didn't realise it would be so high.'

' " Tall and straight, with a proud head to it ",' he quoted. 'That's how sugar ought to be. We'll have a good yield this season. I like to hear the wind in it,' he admitted. 'It gives it a kind of personality, like the sea.'

As they listened to the faint murmur of the cane she understood what he meant and again she was reminded of these few moments on the deck of the *Carmelita* when the wind had stirred the rigging and the waves had whispered along the schooner's hull. It was something she would remember for a very long time because on that occasion Maxwell Rossiter had seemed a different being. At one with the element he loved, he had put everything else behind him, all grudges and hates, all the small, petty things that could clog a man's soul and embitter him for life.

The sea had become a form of escape for him, a free-dom from the tyranny of everyday routine which chained him to La Sola and the growing of sugar cane. Yet she knew without having to be told that he would make a success of that, too.

' When do you harvest the sugar?' she asked.

' In a week or two. Then, all hell will break loose as we cut and grind it. We bring extra labour in from Grenada for a couple of weeks and its pande-monium while it lasts. However, you may enjoy the steel bands and the Limbo dancing, if you haven't seen it before.'

' Only Tom's effort at Limbo last night!'

' Tom will grow up one of these days,' he said.

' He's not very sure about going to Cambridge.'

She was sorry as soon as she had made the observa-tion. Max frowned.

' Tom isn't very sure about anything,' he said. ' He would prefer to drift.'

' At his age, did you really know what you wanted to do?' she challenged.

' I had no option.' He said it with a brief smile. ' My father was alive then and sugar it was!'

When he spoke in this way he reminded her of Alex.

' But there was scope for your love of the sea as well,' she pointed out.

' Certainly. We were never without a boat to sail,' he acknowledged. ' That may have been the encourage-ment I needed for my piratical tendencies.'

She wasn't quite sure whether he was laughing at her or not, but he was evidently well aware of the image he had acquired in the Islands. Perhaps he had even cultivated it.

' Are you chartering the *Carmelita*?' she asked.

He shook his head.

' It's far too big. I'm going up in her to St Vincent and then on to Martinique to pick up one of my yachts to take her to Antigua. English Harbour is my northern headquarters and we winter the yachts there. You'd like Falmouth. It's one of the showpieces of the Caribbean, bursting with history.

Her pulses stirred immediately at the idea of sailing those romantic waters.

'I can imagine,' she agreed, 'but, as I've said before, I'm here to work, and Alex seems to be allergic to the sea.'

The mention of his brother's name seemed to drain all the kindness out of him.

'We're running short of time,' he reminded her, glancing at his wrist watch. 'I dare say you'll want a bath before dinner.'

It was absurd to feel that she had been dismissed, but Vanessa did feel it as she walked back along the corridor. Max's tone had been little short of arbitrary and she resented it.

Barbie was putting Robin to bed, a fact which he also resented to judge by his howls of protest.

'See what's wrong,' Alex said, coming in from the garden.

Vanessa hurried towards the scene of the commotion.

'He want to go with Mister Max tomorrow,' Barbie informed her, 'but Mistress Rossiter she say " no, not this time ", and so it has to be. Mister Max, he away too long in Antigua, maybe.'

Robin was in the tiny bathroom annex to the nursery, running the shower to drown their conversation.

'I *am* going!' he bawled. 'I surely am!'

'Robbie, come out here,' Vanessa called to him. 'I've a proposition to make to you.'

The shower was turned off.

'What's a proposition?' he demanded.

'A suggestion—a bargain, perhaps.'

'I want to go on the schooner!'

'Yes, I know, but your grandmother thinks it's too far. Besides—' She hesitated, then added firmly: 'I think your father would like to take you out. He hasn't seen you for a very long time, so perhaps we could go fishing, or take a picnic somewhere. Tom ought to be able to come, too, before he goes back to

Barbados.'

'He's going to England.' The small voice was suddenly plaintive. Everyone seemed to be leaving the island, everyone he loved. 'I could go with Uncle Max very well.'

'Not this time, Robbie.'

He appeared at the shower-room door, eyeing her with deep suspicion.

'Uncle Max doesn't like you,' he said with a bluntness which reminded her instantly of Max. 'He said you were just another woman.'

'That wasn't very kind of him.' Vanessa bit her lip. 'I'm sure he didn't mean it.'

'Uncle Max always means what he says.'

'And he did say that you had to stay behind this time?'

He nodded, his lips tightly compressed, his finely-marked brows drawn above the amazingly dark eyes.

'Which means that he must have a very good reason for not taking you,' Vanessa pointed out quickly.

'He's going on a charter.'

'Yes, I know, so you couldn't really go, could you? It's business as far as your uncle is concerned. An all-male fishing trip, I have no doubt,' she added a little dryly.

Barbie had hustled Robin into his cotton pyjamas.

'Could we go to the reef?' he asked, having considered Vanessa's proposition in depths.

'I dare say. Shall we ask your father in the morning?'

Robin nodded half-reluctantly, still not very sure about Alex.

'I'd rather go on the schooner,' he said, drawing the bedcover over his head.

'What about your prayers?' Barbie wanted to know.

'I forgot.'

'Then out you come!' Vanessa insisted, feeling a deep affection for this lonely little boy who wanted to be constantly with Maxwell Rossiter, whom he loved.

Robin knelt by the bed, saying the prayer his grandmother had taught him. He had a clear, precise enunciation which was very attractive, reminding her of Helena.

When he was finally tucked in for the night his grandmother came to the nursery door.

'What a row I heard!' she admonished. 'I thought we had a baby in the house.'

'I'm nearly five!' A dark eye peeped at her from a corner of the bedcover. 'We're going to the reef tomorrow, but I'd rather go on the schooner.'

'Another time,' Helena promised, tucking in the cover. 'Another time, my rebellious little love!'

There was compassion as well as affection in her tone and, as she turned away, a hint of an old sorrow in her eyes.

Vanessa went slowly along the corridor to her own room where she showered and changed into a long white skirt and cotton blouse. She felt cooler now and ready for the evening before her.

It was something of a dinner party by the time they were all assembled on the verandah, with the lamps lit and huge moths fluttering to their doom above the flames. There were candles on the dining-table in the room behind them, but they were not yet lit and deep shadows lay between the heavy furniture and slanted along the walls. Max had invited Jacob Bradley, the plantation foreman, to share their meal and the doctor was already seated beside Helena when Vanessa joined them.

Jacob Bradley was a small, compact man in his late fifties with a quick smile which illumined his sun-burned face and a way of referring to Helena which delighted her. In 'the old days' he had served her husband well and although he was almost sixty years of age Max had not pensioned him off. He continued to run the plantation in the way he always had done, with a few modern improvements in the way of machinery which Max had supplied, but fundamentally he was the past, as far as Helena was concerned. He was her link with yesterday, someone of her own generation whom she had come to trust.

Max had not yet come in and Alex poured the

drinks.   He offered Vanessa a long daiquiri in a frosted glass.

'You look radiant,' he said.   'What have you been doing with yourself all day?'

She made a chronicle of the day's events for his benefit, omitting to mention her encounter with Max in the bay.   She did tell him, however, about the library.

'I offered to move your brother's books and papers to the small room at the end of the corridor leading to the garden,' she explained.   'I thought it was the least I could do since we were taking over his former study.'

'The library was always family,' Alex returned shortly.   'My father never made a fetish of keeping it as his particular holy-of-holies.   Don't worry about Max,' he added.   'He'll be perfectly happy shut away there at the end of the garden corridor.   The people he associates with can come and go there without having to pass through the house.'

'What do you mean by the "people he associates with"?' she found herself asking.

Alex looked beyond her towards the door.

'I don't think I need to explain,' he said.

Vanessa turned to find Max standing in the dining-room doorway with another man.

'That's Nick Milford,' Alex informed her.   'A buccaneer, if ever I saw one!'

Nick Milford certainly looked the part.   All he needed, Vanessa thought swiftly, was a cutlass between his teeth.   He was as tall as Max, with broad shoulders and narrow hips, but here the resemblance ceased. Milford slouched where Max walked tall, and his small, close-set eyes peered from a heavily-bearded face. He came across the verandah with his hands in his pockets and an insolent smile on his lips, and it took only a glance in Helena's direction to convince Vanessa that he was not liked.

'Mr Milford,' Helena said coldly, 'we were not expecting you.'

'Max asked me to come along.'   There was an easy

81

familiarity in the man's tone which was surprising. 'We're going on our separate ways in the morning and we have—things to talk about.'

'I dare say,' Helena acknowledged, turning her back on him. 'Alex will get you something to drink.'

One extra guest would mean very little to the catering at La Sola, Vanessa realised, and she could not imagine Helena telling anyone they were not welcome, yet she had made it almost plain on this occasion. Why?

Doctor Nagle directed the conversation into other channels and by the time they filed into the dining-room at ten o'clock the atmosphere had returned to normal. Vanessa sat between Alex and Jacob Bradley, with the doctor, Tom and Nick Milford opposite. Max was at the foot of the table, while Helena took her accustomed place at its head.

The meal was a delight. Little tree-oysters were served in polished shells, followed by iced melon, broiled snapper in lime juice and roast chicken served with breadfruit and mashed yams. With their coffee they had sugar apples and little iced comfits made by one of the cooks. During the meal and, afterwards, as they sat on the verandah again listening to the chirp of the crickets and the guttural croaking of bullfrogs, Vanessa was conscious of Nick Milford watching her intently. His small, amber-coloured eyes seldom left her face and she felt uneasy every time she had to look away from that concentrated stare. He was a man who had very little to talk about apart from his calling. The sea was in his blood and he thought of nothing else, apparently. When he finally rose to go he looked across the verandah to where Max stood beside the rail.

'If I could have a word,' he said, glancing towards the now darkened dining-room. 'I'd like to get back to the bay.'

When he had thanked Helena for her hospitality with a smile which suggested that he knew quite well how she felt about him, Max followed him into the house.

'They'll be closeted in the library for some time, I dare say,' Alex remarked as he stretched his long limbs from the cane chair nearest Vanessa. 'Would you like to take a walk?'

'Your mother—'

'Once she sees the doctor on his way she'll go to bed so that she can be up early in the morning to say good-bye to Max.'

Helena and Doctor Nagle were already on their feet and Tom had disappeared with Jacob Bradley, who had promised him some book or other. The night was still warm, with a bright moon overhead making a pathway of light across the lagoon and it seemed a pity to go to bed. They could hear the wind stirring in the sugar cane, but it was no more than the softest of sighs.

Alex led the way through the banana grove to the beach. The huge, ragged leaves above their heads were edged with silver in the moonlight, but the wind hardly moved them. They hung, limp and motionless, on the terraced slopes, with their gigantic green bunches of fruit thrusting upwards on their thick stems looking oddly macabre in the uncertain light.

'What did you think of Milford?' Alex asked.

'I hardly spoke to him at all.'

'Yet you certainly impressed him.'

'I don't think so. He was just—curious.'

'Is that what you call it? I think he wanted to know all about you.'

'Why should he?'

Alex hesitated.

'He might see you as a distraction, another interest for Max.'

'That's preposterous!'

'I wonder.' Alex helped her down the final terrace on to the soft, unresisting sand. 'When things went wrong for Max,' he added on an indrawn breath, 'he relied on Nick Milford to some extent. Nick was the expert who knew all about the sea and chartering for a living and heaven knows what else, while Max had sufficient money in his pocket to indulge his whims. Now they've enlarged these small beginnings into a

83

profitable partnership. Don't think for one minute that cane and a few acres of cocoa keep my mother in the luxury to which she was accustomed all her life. Max and Milford between them have something else up their sleeves.'

Vanessa hastened across the sand to the edge of the lagoon, wishing that Alex wouldn't talk so frequently about his brother in such derogatory terms. Whatever Max was doing to make a living—chartering or running his freighters at a tremendous profit—she felt that he was doing it honestly enough, although why she should take his part, even in her own thoughts, she did not know.

' At least your mother is comfortable,' she said, ' and that's the main thing. Max takes good care of her.'

Alex strode across the wet sand beside her without answering and presently they reached the far end of the beach where two cottages lay in the shadow of the rocks. The first one was larger than it looked from La Sola.

' An aunt of mine used to live here,' Alex explained. ' My father built it for her when she was first widowed and she still comes across from Barbados occasionally. Mother and Aunt Carrie get on very well, so I expect you'll meet her while you're here.'

' You haven't thought about starting work yet?'

' Maybe in a day or two.' He glanced down at her, seeing her upturned face silvered by the moonlight. ' There's plenty of time, don't you think?'

' It's up to you to say.'

' I've been working like a slave these past few years.'

' Don't tell me you didn't enjoy it!' She was conscious of a tension between them which she sought to dispel with light repartee. ' All authors love their work more than anything else.'

' How would you know that?' He stopped before they came to the shadow of the cottages and his hands fastened tightly over her arms as she turned towards him. ' Of course, I've loved my work, but not more than being conscious of what I've missed in other directions.'

Vanessa stiffened. She didn't want to fall in love with Alex Rossiter, she told herself, and anyway, he was already married. She looked steadfastly into his admiring eyes.

'What about Diane?' she asked.

It was as if she had struck him an unexpected blow across the face. Releasing her, he turned away, scowling.

'She could be dead, for all I know,' he muttered.

'Or care?' She asked the question in spite of herself and it was several seconds before he answered her.

'I've given up hoping she'll ever come back,' he admitted. 'At first—'

She waited, silent in the presence of his bitterest memory.

'At first there was just a chance,' he continued slowly. 'We quarrelled about such a trivial thing, really, and I thought she would change her mind about going. I thought she would beg my forgiveness. That was the measure of my arrogance, I suppose, but she never did. Then there was Robin. For a long time I imagined that she couldn't live without her son, but that, too, was a myth.' He straightened his shoulders, all the emotion blanked out of his face. 'Why are we worrying about it now?' he demanded. 'It's over, gone for ever, a big passion that crumbled into dust. I've forgotten about Diane.'

Vanessa didn't believe him. The extent of his involvement had been there in his eyes for her to read a moment or two ago, the bleak loneliness she had read between the lines of his last novel which he had conveyed to paper so adequately that she could only believe him still in love. However he might deny it, Diane was still in his heart.

In silence they retraced their steps across the moonlit beach, the coral sand softly resisting beneath their feet, the warmth of the tropic night enfolding them. Visibility was straight to the horizon and they could see clearly across the lagoon to the dark outline of the Bluff and beyond it to the bay where the *Carmelita* lay ready to carry Maxwell Rossiter off to a new adventure. The twin masts of the schooner came into view as they climbed above the banana grove, black against the pearl-grey sky, and suddenly Max was there, standing on the Bluff above them. He had come from the direction of the bay and he must surely have seen them walking beside the lagoon.

'He's been seeing Nick Milford off the premises,' Alex reflected. 'I've a feeling there's an uneasy truce between these two. They don't particularly like each other, but they work together because it's necessary. Milford's a good skipper and Max is building up his charter fleet all the time. He needs a knowledgeable man, but whether Milford is trustworthy I wouldn't know. My brother would tell me that it was none of my business, in any case.'

'He's very concerned about your mother,' Vanessa murmured.

'We all are. That's one of the reasons why I came home.'

And the other might be Diane, Vanessa thought.

Max remained standing on the Bluff until they reached the edge of the garden, where there could be no doubt about them being seen from his high vantage point, but instead of coming towards them he turned abruptly away. Whenever he could, he avoided his brother.

'He was engaged to Diane,' Alex said almost reluctantly. 'Although heaven alone knows what they had in common. Perhaps she was a fire in his blood, too. Anyway, it was all over as soon as we met.' He laughed harshly. 'Are you thinking in your little Puritan mind, Vanessa, that I got my just deserts?' he demanded.

'I was thinking about Max,' she admitted. 'His part in all this. If he lost—someone like Diane, someone he loved very much, no wonder he doesn't want to trust another woman ever again.'

'Is that what he told you?'

'Oh, no!' she protested. 'We're hardly on speaking terms. You must know that.'

He looked at her long and searchingly.

86

' Don't go overboard for Max,' he warned, ' or you'll get badly hurt. He has no room for a woman in his life. Not now.'

CHAPTER IV

The following morning Max sailed away in the
Carmelita. Vanessa, who was an early riser, saw the
tall masts of the schooner moving close under the Bluff
as she turned out to sea. She was on a north-westerly
course and would probably be in St Vincent by
nightfall.

If Max was going to St Vincent, she thought. There
were so many islands in the path of the trade winds
and Max hadn't given them any real assurance about
his final destination. He had mentioned one charter
which would take him to Antigua, but he had not said
exactly where he would part with Nick Milford.
Somewhere along their route, she supposed, wondering why it should concern her.

Robin was in the doldrums at breakfast because he
had been left behind, but Alex seized his opportunity
and offered to take him fishing. Tom, who was due
back in Bridgetown at the beginning of the following
week, was completely in agreement.

'What about you, Vanessa?' Alex asked, turning to
her as they left the dining-room. 'Would you like to
come?'

'I promised to move Max's books from the library.'
Vanessa had to keep reminding herself that Alex had
brought her to this delightful island to work. 'I said
I would take them along to his den and he could sort
them out later. Besides, there's your mother. I'd like
to stay with her, if you don't mind.'

'I don't mind at all,' he informed her almost
sharply, 'but you don't have to work for Max, you
know. He won't appreciate you any the more if you
grovel.'

She bit her lip on the retort which sprang to mind.

'I'll stay, all the same,' she decided. 'If there's any
typing you want done, I can tackle it first.'

'I've more revision to do on the first chapters,' he
said distantly. 'It will take time.'

'Yes, of course.'

Robin considered her solemnly as they went out towards the car.

'If you come, too,' he offered, 'I could show you where to fish.'

Her face lit with a warm smile.

'Another time, Robbie,' she agreed.

When they had gone she knocked on Helena's door.

'Come in!'

Helena was sitting up in bed while Barbie fussed around, tidying the room.

'That will do, Barbie,' she decided. 'You can take my tray now. I've enjoyed my breakfast.'

Barbie's face creased in a delighted grin.

'I glad you enjoy it, mistress.' She took it as a personal compliment. 'You sure need fattening up.'

Helena looked across at her visitor and smiled.

'Barbie would see me as fat as a porker,' she declared. 'Did you watch the schooner go out?'

Presented with the thought of Max again, Vanessa nodded.

'From a distance.'

'Max is always on the go from first light. He says it's the best part of the day.' Helena settled back among her pillows. 'I used to think so, too, but now I'm told to rest, and Max is as stern a taskmaster in that respect as Albert Nagle. They tell me I have nothing else to do, and that, to a woman who has been active all her life, is more or less a death knell. These past few years I've been able to help Max a lot, taking charge of the paper work in connection with the estate, but now he thinks it is too much for me.'

'It's something I could do,' Vanessa offered impulsively. 'If Max agreed.'

'He told me you'd offered to clear the library for him.' Helena looked pleased. 'He works too hard, every hour of the day, which isn't good for anyone. Oh, I know he makes a lot of money, but that isn't everything. It keeps us comfortable, I admit, but it can warp a man's sense of proportion. Max should take time off to play occasionally. Quite often I worry about him.'

'Isn't the sea his great relaxation?' Vanessa suggested.

'He makes that pay, too.' Helena indicated the chair beside her bed. 'He's terribly independent,' she added, still thinking of Max as Vanessa sat down, 'but his heart's in the right place. I want you to like him,' she added unexpectedly.

'I don't want to intrude,' Vanessa confessed, 'but I would like to help. It rather looks as if Alex won't start work properly for a day or two, so I feel that I'm here under false pretences at present.'

'I'm glad he's gone off with Robin,' Helena said, looking beyond her. 'The child has seen all too little of him recently. A boy needs a man's influence in his life, even at Robin's age, and Max is often away, too. He also needs a younger woman about the place,' she added thoughtfully. 'I'm too old and infirm to look after him properly and Barbie spoils him. When you start on the library,' she added briefly, 'I'll give you a hand. Max has far more stuff stowed away in there than he realises, so we'll sort it out together.'

'You're sure it won't be too much for you?'

'Not at all! I'll enjoy your company for an hour and we'll have tea together afterwards.'

Vanessa worked hard all morning. Helena's estimate of her self-imposed task in clearing Max's books had not been exaggerated. The volumes of reference he had put to one side for his own use were almost equal in number to those already adorning the shelves which stretched from floor to ceiling on two sides of the room, and she was more than glad of Joe's help. The young Negro boy had been sent in from the plantation to assist her, and he carried the heavier books while she attended to the files which had been heaped in a haphazard pile on the desk. Others had found a temporary resting-place on the broad window-seat or on the floor itself. She had noticed a filing cabinet in the smaller room and was not greatly surprised to find it empty.

'I'll file these,' she told Joe, 'while you fetch the

other books from the library. It won't take long.'

While she worked she could look out across the garden to the sugar plantation and, beyond it, to the hills. It was an utterly different view from the one which they enjoyed from the verandah, but she fancied that it would be one Max would enjoy. Where the sugar ended the hills rose sharply on either side of the valley floor, culminating in a serrated edge of rock which Joe told her had once been a mountain.

'Big bang came long time ago an' blew him away,' he explained, round-eyed with awe. 'He blew top right off him head.'

'A volcano?'

Joe nodded.

'He no good volcano now.' The black eyes were full of scorn. 'He jus' big hole in mountain.'

Most of the Caribbean islands were volcanic in origin and this one was no exception, but it seemed that the danger from a new eruption was negligible. The thought of their resident volcano held its own strange attraction for Vanessa, however, and she could easily imagine how imposing the distant mountain had looked before 'he blew top right off him head'. On a warm day it would be cool up there above the tree line, with the gentle trade wind blowing against one's cheeks, and it would be easy enough to climb after the sugar was left behind. One day she would try it, she thought, and perhaps Tom—or Alex—would go with her. She could imagine Max climbing the mountain, too, but always alone.

Helena came along the corridor fresh from her afternoon siesta.

'You've almost finished!' she exclaimed, glancing round the tidy room. 'You must have worked very hard.'

'I had Joe to help me,' Vanessa smiled. 'He's a mine of information. I understand you once had a resident volcano.'

'A long while ago.' Helena crossed to her side. 'Joe could only have heard about it from his parents, because it blew long before he was born. Perhaps they wanted to scare him away from the summit. It's no place for children.'

The bluff which ran out between the bay and the lagoon was the extended foot of the mountain and they could just see the edge of it from where they stood at the window.

'Max has a wonderful view of the hills from here,' Helena observed. 'No wonder he likes it. Into the bargain, it's isolated enough for him to work in peace and to come and go as he likes.'

Vanessa could imagine Max using the garden door from now on. He could come straight up from the bay to the house without being observed from the verandah and he could leave in the same way when he sought to avoid them.

'I still feel that we deprived him of the library,' she murmured half apologetically. 'I could have worked quite well on my verandah.'

'You needn't worry about Max,' Helena answered. 'He only works inside when he has to, and one room is as good as another as far as he is concerned. You've filed everything so neatly,' she reflected, pulling open one of the cabinet drawers. 'I hope he'll appreciate the fact.'

'I don't want him to feel obliged to me,' Vanessa protested. 'It was just as easy to file the papers as to leave them lying on the floor.'

Helena nodded.

'Bachelors develop an untidy streak,' she sighed. 'Max needs a wife to keep him in line.' She sat down at her son's desk. 'I'd like to see all my sons married before I go,' she added, 'but happily married. Is that too much to ask?'

'I don't think so.'

'Max was in love once, but he never speaks of Diane now. She was a very beautiful girl, half French, half Spanish, a fireball, always searching for something new, never content. She was very young, of course, when Max first brought her here from Martinique. They were engaged to be married.' She sighed once more. 'Maybe if Alex hadn't come along things might have turned out all right, but maybe it just had to be. I try to be philosophical about it, but sometimes when I look at Max and think about Alex's changed way of life I wonder why one woman should be allowed to wreck a whole family. There's Robin, too. He shouldn't be running wild the way he does, sailing off with Max whenever he'll take him without a woman's influence somewhere in the background. I try to apply a firm hand, but since my illness, I've not been able to take control. That's why I'd like another woman around the place—permanently.'

Vanessa knew that Max would never marry for such a reason, although he appeared to be inordinately fond of Robin. Because of Diane? The man loving the child because of the woman he had once loved—or still loved?

The thought shattered her because, suddenly, she knew that she could have loved this man. From the moment of their first meeting in Barbados Maxwell Rossiter had attracted her as no other man had ever done. He had none of his brother's superficial charm, he had been almost brutally antagonistic from the moment they had met, yet there was a strength and purpose about him which she could admire. But it was all quite hopeless, she told herself, and best forgotten.

She closed the drawer which Helena had opened.

'One day he may marry,' she said harshly. 'Surely one isolated incident in the past can't close his mind to kindness and—love for ever.'

'I hope not.' Helena got up from the desk. 'Here come Robbie and Alex,' she added, looking through the window. 'They seem to have had a wonderful day.'

Surprisingly Robin came in by the garden door while Alex walked round the house with the fishing tackle to deliver their catch at the kitchens.

'Robbie!' his grandmother exclaimed, 'did you have to go in after the fish right over your head? Just look at you! You're covered in mud. What was your father thinking about?'

93

'He got me out when I fell in the pond,' Robin explained with a complete lack of regard for his danger, 'but I could've swimmed out the way Uncle Max told me.'

'Maybe you could, and maybe not,' Helena reminded him. 'It was just as well your father was there.'

Robin considered the point.

'Yes,' he agreed after a pause.

'So, off you go and clean up,' Helena commanded. 'Barbie will help you.'

'Let me,' Vanessa offered. 'I'm much in need of a wash myself!' She held out her dusty hands.

Robin looked at his grandmother for confirmation.

'Off you go,' Helena said. 'It will take half the time without Barbie!'

Robin marched along the corridor ahead of Vanessa, his wet sandals squelching on the coco-matting until they reached the bathroom next to the nursery.

'I think you ought to have a shower,' Vanessa suggested. 'It would be much the easiest way.'

While she helped him to take off his clothes he studied her carefully.

'Are you going to climb the mountain?' he asked.

'The one behind the house?' She shook her head. 'I don't think so, Robbie. Not to-day, anyway.'

'Uncle Max goes right up there, right to the top, when he wants to think.' Robin kicked off his sandals. 'One day I'll go, too.'

'No, Robbie!' Vanessa cried in sudden alarm. 'You mustn't! Not by yourself, anyway.'

A determined look came into the dark eyes, although he made no effort to challenge her.

'I wish my mummy would come back,' he said after a pause.

Vanessa was overwhelmed with pity because Diane could be dead without them knowing.

'Some day she will,' she found herself saying as she turned on the shower.

Their friendship dated from that moment onwards. Wherever she went, Robin followed, plying her with information about La Sola, showing her his favourite hideaways, talking about Max. In his uncle's absence he accompanied her everywhere, and when Tom returned to Bridgetown at the beginning of the following week he was her sole companion. Alex had decided to work. He shut himself up in the library during the mornings, swam with them for an hour in the afternoons and then went back to his manuscript.

Helena rested most of the time, as Max and Doctor Nagle had decreed, but she was always up and seated in her favourite chair on the verandah by tea time.

When the schooner came back into the bay she was first to notice it.

' There's the *Carmelita!*' she said. ' Max has come home.'

Vanessa knew that it could just as easily be Nick Milford who had brought the schooner in, but her heart began to race as she stood at the verandah rail, watching.

The *Carmelita* dropped anchor, but it was another hour before a small boat pulled away from her side.

Robin tugged at Vanessa's hand.

' Please can we go?' he begged. ' Can we go to meet Uncle Max?'

Vanessa looked round at Helena to surprise an odd expression in her eyes.

' Why not?' she asked. ' You could take him down to the bay, otherwise there will be no peace till Max gets here.'

Vanessa hesitated. Alex was still busy; he had not come to the verandah to take tea with them, preferring to have it sent in to the library on a tray, which suggested that he was still concentrating on his revision. So far he had not asked for her help, but she supposed that he would expect her to work at pressure when the manuscript came to be typed.

Robin tugged at her hand.

'Come on!' he urged. ' We'll be late.'

Whoever had brought the schooner back to the bay would be ashore by now, and if it was Max she could easily imagine his irritation when he saw her. He would resent her being there, even if she had Robin to present as her excuse.

'Please can we hurry?' Robin was half-way along the verandah. 'We might easily miss him.'

Vanessa followed the diminutive figure down the steps.

'Watch how you go,' Helena called, 'if you take the short-cut over the Bluff.'

It was the way Max invariably came when he returned alone to La Sola from the bay, but they were taking a chance of missing him if he had company. He would come by the road, in that case, but by now Vanessa was almost hoping that they would miss him.

Robin ran ahead of her up the incline to the Bluff. The path was a steep one, made slippery by a recent downpour of rain, but he was as nimble as a mountain goat and as intent on his purpose. Max would never have a more faithful devotee.

When they finally pushed through the brush at the top of the pathway the whole bay on the other side opened out before them. A great deal of activity was going on around the group of huts which formed the village: stores were being carried shoulder-high across the beach and the launch was surrounded by a horde of native women in gay print dresses with baskets on their heads, ready to assist their menfolk. Scantily-clad children frolicked in the surf, their brown bodies glistening as they stretched their hands up to the jetty for their quota of sweetmeats. Even from where Vanessa stood she could hear their laughter and something about the primitive little scene awakened a response in her. At least, Max's return seemed to be appreciated by the people who depended on him for their livelihood.

Robin was already on his way down the Bluff and she was forced to follow him. Long before they had reached the jetty she knew that Max had brought the schooner in. She could see his tall figure, head and shoulders, above the natives as he issued his orders and even from that distance he seemed to dominate the scene.

As soon as the soft white sand was underneath his feet Robin took flight. He ran heedlessly along the beach, falling twice in his precipitous race for the jetty, and she saw Max lift him shoulder-high to swing him into the launch.

Her own progress was slower, and she even wondered if she should turn back now that Robin was safely in his uncle's keeping. A desperate shyness assailed her and her steps lagged in the warm coral sand, but Max had already seen her. Robin was pointing along the beach, obviously explaining that he had not come all that way alone.

Crushing back her ridiculous nervousness, she walked steadily towards the jetty. Whatever Max might think about their meeting, she wasn't going to be intimidated by his disapproval.

The native women stood aside to let her pass, but she could sense their curiosity. Most of them already knew about her arrival on the island and their round black eyes turned to Max in surprise. In their language she was 'Alex's woman', she supposed, because Alex Rossiter had brought her to La Sola, and here she was meeting Alex's brother in broad daylight for all to see. There were coy smiles and meaningful looks which made it all the harder for her to meet Max with equanimity.

The launch was unloaded and he was about to come ashore; she knew that there would be no hope of persuading Robin to return to La Sola without him. If Max had been surprised when he had first seen her walking along the beach he was in full command of his emotions by the time they were face to face. He regarded her in silence.

'Robin wanted to come down,' she explained unnecessarily. 'We were having tea on the verandah when your mother saw the *Carmelita* come in.'

'How is she?' he asked without making any reference to her rather lame explanation of her presence on the jetty.

'She's rested a lot, and I'm sure that makes a difference. She really has stayed in her room all morning.'

'Under protest, I've no doubt.' The sun glinted on several days' growth of black beard as he turned to issue a final order to the native crew. 'I've brought one or two things back for her to ease the boredom. She's like a child where presents are concerned.'

'Who isn't?' Vanessa felt the tension between them easing a little. 'It looks as if Robin has been lucky, too.'

'He always has a nose for a parcel.' His stern mouth relaxed as his nephew came to stand on the gunwale of the launch. 'Do you think you can carry that load over the Bluff?' he asked.

Robin nodded. His arms were full and one of the seamen had to lift him from the launch. Max slung a canvas bag over his shoulder as he turned towards the beach.

'Are you tired?' he asked.

'Not in the slightest.' Vanessa was more than ready to walk back to La Sola with him. 'I haven't been doing much all day, except reading.'

'I thought you and Alex would be up to your eyes in work by now.'

'Alex is,' she told him as they set off along the sand, 'but he isn't quite ready for me yet. He had a lot of revision to do. I've transferred all your books,' she added hastily when he did not reply. 'I hope you'll find everything as you want it.'

'I'm an untidy person where papers are concerned,' he admitted. 'Surely you've noticed that by now.'

Vanessa smiled.

'I have, as a matter of fact, and I've done some filing for you. The files were there, so why not? Your room isn't as big as the library and I thought it looked tidier with everything in the cabinet. You seem to have a lot of paper work to catch up on.'

'It's the bane of my existence,' he confessed. 'My mother used to take some of it off my hands, but I can't ask her just now while she isn't completely fit.'

'Supposing you asked me?' Vanessa suggested. 'At least till Alex is ready for me.'

'That would be out of the question,' he said.

'Why?'

'You didn't come to La Sola to work for me.'

'It would be for the estate,' she pointed out.

'All the same, I think Alex would object.'

'Why should he?'

'On principle, perhaps.'

The words silenced her, refreshing the memory of their enmity which seemed to govern all their contacts these days. It might have been different once—before Max had brought Diane to the island.

Robin came back to walk beside them.

'Do you want to put your parcels in the sack?' Max asked.

'Yes, please—except this one.' He held up a miniature tractor which had escaped from its paper wrapping. 'I can bring in the sugar now,' he added proudly.

'Some of it,' Max agreed with a grin. 'Later on you'll be able to drive a real one.'

No man could have spoken to his own son more tenderly; he loved this child who had been brought up at La Sola under his care, but he had also never allowed Robin to forget his mother. The little boy had spoken about Diane quite naturally, wishing that she would return.

They came to the end of the sand where the rocks sloped down from the Bluff and Robin ran on ahead to find the narrow path which led through the undergrowth to the top. It was a fairly stiff climb, but Max made no effort to help her, and Vanessa was determined to keep pace with him. As he strode ahead to clear the ramblers from their path he looked every inch a buccaneer, the effect suitably heightened by the black beard and the sack slung over his shoulder. She saw him silhouetted against the sea when they reached the top, that blue Caribbean Sea which he knew so well. He knew the tidal streams as well as he knew the calms and the sudden frenzy of the winds which swept towards the Gulf before a storm, and she recognised it as part of his life, the part he would not relinquish even for La Sola and the good of the estate. One day, she thought, if Alex did decide to settle here, Max would take to the sea for good. Only his mother and her welfare kept him at La Sola now.

From the ridge of the Bluff they could look down on the house and the banana plantation and the cane fields stretching along the valley floor like a waving green sea. It was all so quiet and peaceful until, suddenly, Alex was standing there on the path before them, his face convulsed with anger.

'Where the devil have you been?' he demanded, fixing Vanessa with a hard stare. 'I was ready to begin work an hour ago.'

'I didn't know.' She felt the hot colour of embarrassment running up under her skin. 'Robin wanted to meet the schooner and I couldn't let him go alone.'

'What was the matter with Barbie or one of the others?' Alex demanded. 'There are plenty of women around the place, heaven knows! I didn't employ you as a nurse for Robin.'

Max shifted the sack to his other shoulder.

'It's almost six o'clock,' he pointed out. 'If you must behave like a temperamental author, Alex, I'd do it in office hours, if I were you.'

Alex glared at him.

'I haven't asked your advice,' he retorted cuttingly. 'You seem to have come back before you were expected. What happened?'

'Nothing specific.' Max walked on. 'I brought the *Carmelita* in because I suddenly made up my mind not to go to Antigua this trip. Nick is capable enough.'

'I'm sure,' Alex agreed dryly. 'What was his cargo this time?'

'Americans.'

They could see no more than the back of his head, but Vanessa sensed how angry Max was. He was trying to keep his temper with Alex, but his brother was making it difficult for him.

'Another charter?' Alex mused. 'You seem to be doing well in that direction.'

'Reasonably so. It's something which evolved quite naturally out of the freighters and the original sloop.' Max had caught up with Robin. 'Race you!' he offered. 'First to the house gets a chocolate bar!'

Alex stood his ground on the path.

'Look here, Vanessa,' he said a trifle sheepishly, 'I didn't mean to bawl you out, but—'

'I must have deserved it.' Vanessa tried to smile. 'I realise now that I should have told you where I was going.'

'I can't expect to take up all your time,' he growled.

'You can expect me to work when I'm needed,' she acknowledged, 'but I honestly did think you weren't ready for me. I had tea with your mother and we saw the schooner come in.'

'Which meant that Robin had to rush down to the bay,' he finished for her. 'I know. Max has made himself indispensable to the boy.'

A note of deep resentment had crept into his voice, or it could have been envy. Vanessa could not be sure, but what she did know was that Max had not deliberately cultivated Robin's adoration.

'It's a natural sequence, isn't it?' she said as they followed the two racing figures through the garden. 'A boy needs a man's influence at Robbie's age more than at any other time.'

'You could be right,' her employer conceded. 'I may have stayed away too long.'

One again Vanessa felt incredibly sorry for him.

'It's something you could easily remedy,' she suggested.

'By staying put?' He looked trapped for a moment. 'I'd never be able to live under the same roof as Max,' he decided.

Perhaps that was sadly true, Vanessa thought. The division between them was too great, the hurt Alex had inflicted on his younger brother too deep to be erased.

'If you want me to begin work right away,' she offered, 'I will. I've been lazing around for two weeks now, doing nothing.'

'You've been getting to know my mother and La Sola,' he pointed out. 'No, Max was right. I've no reason to throw a temperamental fit when I find myself thwarted. We'll start work in the morning, bright and early. How fast can you type?'

'Around fifty words a minute when I try hard enough!'

'You needn't go flat out,' he grinned. 'I'll settle for less than that since you'll have to take a hard look at my spelling occasionally.'

They were back on the old footing; Alex had forgotten his frustration and some of his vexation with Max.

Vanessa discovered how easy it was to work for him over the next few days while they occupied the library from ten in the morning until tea-time. Helena insisted that they should stop at four o'clock and by that time Vanessa was quite ready to relax. She swam in the lagoon in the early morning. The water was shallow and always warm, and sometimes Alex joined her, but Max preferred to go in on the far side of the Bluff, where the waves were a challenge. He had warned her against the currents on that side, but he was a powerful swimmer and so he had the bay to himself.

Robin paddled in the sea most of the day, in and out of the shallow green water, learning new strokes from Alex when he came down early enough but looking enviously towards the Bluff where his uncle swam alone. One day he would be able to bathe there, too, copying Max in everything.

On Sunday they took a picnic lunch to the valley, climbing a little way up the mountainside towards its ragged, serrated summit.

'We used to come up here a lot when we were boys,' Alex reflected. 'It seems a long time ago.'

For a moment Vanessa felt that he was regretting the past and his quarrel with Max, but nothing she could say would help the situation. Sometimes Diane's presence came very near.

Alex got up to scramble across the rocks in Robin's wake.

'We could go to the very top,' Robin suggested eagerly. 'Right up, where the clouds are.'

'It's too far,' Alex decided, 'and it could be dangerous.'

'Uncle Max climbs right to the top.'

'So?' Alex said. 'He's bigger than you.'

'One day I'll go,' Robin boasted. 'When I'm as big as you are.'

He had warmed to Alex in the past few days because his father had had more time to play, and now they were friends. Alex had yet to win his complete confidence, but he seemed content enough to wait.

Two days later he entered the library with a dark frown creasing his brow.

'I have to go to Barbados,' he said, fingering one of the letters which had come for him in the mail. 'If I make a dash for it I can go back with the trader.'

Vanessa looked up from the typewriter.

'Do you want me to go with you?' she asked.

'No.' His reply was hasty. 'I'm going on business.'

He looked down at the letter in his hand and for a moment she thought that he was going to confide in her, but he changed his mind.

'How long will you be away?' she asked.

'I don't know, but you can carry on to chapter six. That's as far as I've got with the revision, I'm afraid. I find it slow work now and again.'

'For lack of inspiration?'

'Not exactly.' He folded the letter and put it into his wallet. 'My mind gets clogged up with other things.'

'Like new ideas?'

He shook his head.

'Old catastrophes.' He tried to smile. 'The past should bury its dead, but it never does.'

She looked down at the pile of typescript on the desk beside her, wanting to ask if the letter had come from Diane but not knowing how. Perhaps someone who had known Diane had written to him and he was going in search of a ghost. He had told her once that he didn't know whether his wife was dead or alive.

'Do you mind if I do some of the estate paper work while you're away?' she asked instead.

' For Max?'

' Your mother used to do it.'

He turned towards the door.

' I've no objection. You should finish those final chapters in a week.'

' You'll wait for the trader coming back?'

' Of course.'

He wouldn't ask Max to fetch him this time, or even to put the schooner at his disposal to cross to Bridgetown, which would save time and be much more convenient.

Vanessa took Robin down to the bay to see him off.

' Is he going away for good?' The small voice was curiously plaintive. ' He said we would have more picnics in the valley.'

' So we shall, Robin,' Vanessa assured him. ' He's just going on business for a day or two.'

The day or two stretched to a week. The trader came in again, but Alex was not among the small group of passengers coming ashore. Vanessa recognised the doctor, who smiled at her, but he was with an elderly lady and they did not speak. Disappointed, they walked back to La Sola. The next trader wouldn't sail in for three more days.

Vanessa had led Robin down to the bay on the donkey and they were half way back to the house when they were overtaken by the ramshackle old car which served the village as its only taxi. It pulled up just ahead of them.

' Hullo, Robbie!' its occupant greeted them. ' Surely you haven't forgotten me?'

' Aunt Carrie!' The child was delighted. ' Did you come with the trader?'

'I did.' The small, chubby woman in the flowered hat got out of the taxi to kiss him, smiling at Vanessa in the meantime. ' Helena wrote me all about you,' she said. ' How are you all? I got anxious about Helena, so I thought I would come over without bothering to tell her. I have the Beach House down on the shore, you know. But I guess Helena's told you.'

'Yes, she has,' Vanessa smiled, liking this gay little lady immediately. 'She said you often arrived out of the blue!'

'I have to get away from Bridgetown now and then,' Carrie admitted. 'The place gets too much for me.' She got back into the taxi. 'Would you care to ride along with me?'

'We've got Rosalind.' Vanessa indicated the donkey. 'I think I'd better walk.'

'I see the schooner is in,' Carrie commented. 'Max must be home.'

'He's been at La Sola for over a week.'

Carrie's fair eyebrows shot up.

'You don't say? Worried about his mother, was he?'

'I think so.'

'I met Alex in Bridgetown.' Carrie gave her a penetrating look. 'Wouldn't say what he was doing there, but he gave me a letter.' She searched in her handbag. 'It's for you,' she said, holding out a long envelope.

'It must be something he wants urgently,' Vanessa guessed, conscious that her cheeks were warm. 'I've finished all the typing he left me to do.'

'Could be,' Carrie agreed. 'On you go, Lucas,' she ordered the native driver. 'My throat's parched for a decent cup of tea.'

Vanessa led the donkey along the dust road, clutching Alex's letter in her hand and wondering what he could have to say to her of some urgency after just one week. She had no opportunity of opening it till they reached the house, but she went straight to her room when she had helped Robin to stable Rosalind. Robin raced on ahead of her towards the verandah where his grandmother was greeting her unexpected guest and Vanessa could hear their chatter as she walked through the deserted house. There was no sign of Max, but at this hour he would probably be in the cane fields. With the harvesting looming up, the activity at La Sola would increase, and that could have been his reason for returning from St Vincent instead of going on to Antigua with the new charter.

Closing her bedroom door, she took Alex's letter from her pocket. It was very much to the point.

'I came here because I had to,' it began without preliminary. 'You must know by now that the thought of Diane is always with me. Everywhere I go I'm conscious that my wife may be somewhere quite near or on the other side of the world. It's nearly two years since any of us has heard of her or from her; she could be dead, but every now and then some kind friend writes to me saying he thinks he has seen her. Mostly I arrive to find myself at a dead end. This has been one of them. If Diane was here, she has moved on, possibly with the gay crowd she prefers to La Sola, but I have to go on making the effort to trace her, mostly for Robin's sake. She should be with her son some of the time, don't you think?'

'Forget that last question,' the letter ran on. 'It means I'm involving you and I don't want to do that. Not just now. I'm writing to tell you to go ahead with the next chapter of my book. I won't alter it and I hope to come back with the next freighter. How are the accounts going? Don't let Max work you too hard. I saw the doctor go over on the trader with Aunt Carrie, so I expect he's looking after Mother. Aunt Carrie will keep you all amused.

'Alex.'

Vanessa stood looking at the brief signature for a long time after she had finished reading her employer's letter, aware of an implication in Alex's communication which she did not want to accept. 'It means I'm involving you and I don't want to do that—not just now.' She didn't want to be involved; she couldn't be. Alex was married, and whatever Diane had done in the past she had a right to return to La Sola and her son.

Walking through to the verandah, she looked down across the banana plantation to the lagoon where the sun was about to set. She was already involved, she thought desperately. She would be part of this family for the next three months, and even now she was thinking about them as her own, with the possible exception of Max. Max would never belong to anyone. He would go on living his life in his own solitary way, accountable to no one, the dark master of his own fate.

Yet if Diane returned, what then?

She thrust the thought aside, wondering what to say to Helena about Alex's letter because Aunt Carrie was sure to have told her there was one. They were seated on the verandah when she went out.

' You're just in time for some nice, fresh tea,' Helena announced. ' You've already met my sister-in-law, I hear. Carrie drops in on us whenever she can and this time I've persuaded her to stay at La Sola for a day or two while the Beach House is being prepared. The roof was damaged in a storm we had just before you and Alex arrived and the boys are so slow about repairing anything. Of course, it's harvest time,' she allowed, ' and Max needs all the labour in the fields. Soon we will have Carnival again,' she mused.

' I'm determined that my roof will be over my head long before Carnival!' Carrie declared. ' I'm on the spot, now, not miles away in Bridgetown.'

' Carrie gets things done,' Helena smiled, looking much brighter in her sister-in-law's presence. ' She's very much like Max.'

' We get on well enough,' Carrie agreed. ' Max was always my favourite nephew.'

Carrie Hazeltine was the type who would ' get on ' with anyone, Vanessa thought, accepting her tea cup from Alex's mother, and she evidently saw eye to eye with Max because they shared the same vigorous outlook on life. She would also sympathise with Alex because he was not quite sure where he was going from here, but she could not admire him as she admired Max.

Vanessa could feel Alex's uncertainty in spite of the assured, careless face he turned to the world; she could sense his hurt, too, but she could not help him. He had to work out the future for himself.

' Alex sent a letter,' she said, turning back to Helena.

107

'He hopes to come home with the next trader.'

'Another three days,' Helena murmured. 'I wonder what drastic business is keeping him in Barbados. I thought he did his work when and where he pleased.' She glanced in her sister-in-law's direction. 'I hope we're not going to have all that "itchy feet" bit again.'

'I don't think so,' Carrie answered. 'When I met him in Bridgetown yesterday Alex struck me as being much more settled, more mature in every way.'

'So he should be,' Helena replied. 'He's over thirty.'

'One forgets.' Carrie sipped her tea. 'Come down to the Beach House with me in the morning,' she suggested. 'We can take the buggy and the change will do you good. Albert Nagle is coming to see you in the afternoon, so I suppose he means to stay for a couple of days.'

'He's welcome any time,' Helena said. 'You are all most welcome.' Her quick smile included Vanessa. 'I believe much of my trouble was loneliness. An ageing woman on her own takes time out to think about her infirmities.'

'Not you!' Carrie protested. 'Upon my word,' she exclaimed, looking beyond her sister-in-law, 'here comes the master of the house himself, all tricked out as if he's been working!'

Her remark was completely without malice as she looked up at her nephew and Max smiled at her.

'So you kept your word,' he said, kissing her firm, round cheek.

Carrie Hazeltine's pale blue eyes lit with pleasure.

'Did you ever know me not to keep it?' she demanded. 'I said I would come, and here I am. You didn't have to blow my roof off to speed me on my way!'

'I'm seeing to the repairs.' Max sat down on the chair next to his mother. 'The Beach House should be ready for you in under a week.'

'You're like your father,' Carrie said. 'Every inch a Rossiter. Your mother agrees with me.'

'I've no alternative!' Helena laughed, the sparkle

still in her eyes. 'Tea, Max—or are you only passing through?'

'I came up with tea in mind.'

He was far more relaxed now, Vanessa thought, yet she was uneasily aware of the letter in her pocket which Alex had written in Barbados. It had nothing to do with Max, but she was instinctively sure that he would resent it if he knew about it.

'Alex isn't coming back till Friday,' Helena told him. 'He sent word by Carrie.'

No direct mention of who had received the letter, Vanessa noticed, but perhaps that hadn't been really necessary. Max was looking straight at her.

'Robin's overfeeding that donkey of his,' he remarked. 'Maybe we should cut down on her regular meals. I promised Robin I'd take him along next time I went out,' he added, turning back to his mother. 'Wilson is having trouble with the *Charlotte Lucia*, so I'm going over to St Vincent in the morning.'

Helena considered the idea.

'He can't go alone,' she decided. 'He'd get into all sorts of mischief when your back was turned.'

'One of the girls can come along to look after him —Barbie or Francine.'

'Francine is off sick and I just can't spare Barbie.' Helena looked across the verandah at Vanessa. 'Why not?' she said, as if answering her own unspoken question. 'You ought to see as much of the Caribbean as you can, Vanessa, while you are here. Alex can't possibly expect you to work all the time.'

'He has sent me some work to do,' Vanessa said, thereby admitting that she had been the recipient of Alex's letter. 'I'd love to go, of course, but—'

She left the sentence unfinished, conscious that Max was looking at her. It was really his decision whether she should go or not and she was prepared for his refusal. A dark colour stained her cheeks as she waited for him to speak.

'Please can I go? Please, Uncle Max!' a small voice piped up from the shadows behind Helena's chair. 'You said I could, remember?'

'In other circumstances,' Max began.

'What other circumstances?' Carrie wanted to know. I shall be here to look after your mother and Doctor Nagle will be staying till the freighter goes back on Friday afternoon. It's a wonderful opportunity for Miss Gilbert to see our lovely islands. One she shouldn't miss.'

'It's out of the question,' Max scowled.

'Why is it?' Helena spoke for the first time in several minutes, minutes in which she had been studying her son and the girl Alex had brought to La Sola. 'You could take Vanessa and Robin to the Andersons' once you reached Georgetown if you really are going to be too busy to show Vanessa around yourself.'

'Please, Uncle Max!'

With a brow as dark as thunder Max stood contemplating the waving banana fronds. He would have taken Robin, but not 'Alex's woman', not this stranger who had come into their midst without warning, not any woman.

'Maybe I could do without Barbie,' Helena conceded, 'and she's always ready to be off on a jaunt, especially with Robin.'

Vanessa felt that she had been waiting for Max's decision for an eternity.

'Please!' Robin begged once more. 'We could feed Rosalind before we left.'

'Rosalind could quite easily live on her own fat for a week!' Max's brow had cleared a little by the time he turned back to Vanessa. 'Bring Barbie,' he said. 'You may need her.'

The rush of joy she experienced was out of all proportion to his generosity, Vanessa told herself, but she was determined to go. With Barbie there to help with Robin she wouldn't be the only woman on board the schooner.

CHAPTER V

They came to St Vincent the following afternoon as
the sun was setting. The whole sky had taken on a
vivid orange glow radiating upwards from the horizon
to fire the clouds, but it was the great conical mountain
dominating the whole island which caught and held
Vanessa's attention. They were sailing towards Kingstown harbour with the dying sun staining the sides of
Souffrière, and it almost seemed as if the great volcanic
peak was about to erupt once more. Its jagged sides
were almost blood-red as they rounded Young's Island
and came into its shadow for the first time. In 1902
Souffrière had spilled over, burying a town, and ninety
years before that, almost to a day, the volcano had
belched out flame and smoke and burning lava and
dropped three million tons of dust in Barbados, which
was ninety miles away.

Vanessa looked up at the slumbering giant in awe.

'You've got plenty of time,' Max said at her elbow.
'The last eruption was in 1902, and the Carib legends
say that Souffrière only coughs up fire and brimstone
once in ninety years.'

'Time to go away, I suppose you mean?' She
turned to look at this man who resented her merely
because she was a woman. 'I'll have to take my chance
with Souffrière,' she decided, 'and I don't suppose the
fireworks would ever reach La Sola.'

'We have our own resident volcano,' he said, 'long
since subdued.'

She looked towards the bay opening out in front
of them, seeing the clustered town huddling at the foot
of the hills and the steep walls of an ancient fortress
rising several hundred feet above it.

'Fort Charlotte,' Max said for her benefit. 'It
glares seawards across the harbour, but it has never
fired a shot in anger for over a hundred years.'

'I think it looks beautiful,' Vanessa said. 'All these
lovely old houses down there beside the water, with

the fort and the mountains guarding them.'

He hadn't spoken to her much on the way over, but she had been content just to roam the decks with Robin and see that he ate at regular intervals and not just when the spirit moved him or the native cook offered him titbits. Barbie, who had a store of sweetmeats in her possession, would have fed him continuously if she hadn't been watched.

Max had been busy, of course, but now that they were coming into harbour he had time to relax. He leaned his tall, thin form against the rail, his back to the sea.

'In a minute we'll be invaded by the bum-boats,' he warned her. ' You can ignore them or fall victim to their blandishments, just as you please.'

A small flotilla of lighters came rapidly towards the schooner, sculled by their crews in an endeavour to be first at the *Carmelita's* side. Dark faces were turned up towards the deck, black eyes gleamed. Max handed Vanessa a silver coin to toss into the water, watching her delight with amusement as two Negro youths went overboard after it, diving to a great depth to retrieve the gleaming, twisting coin.

' All the tourists oblige,' he said. ' It's been the custom for longer than anyone can remember. They're experts at it, as were their fathers before them, the only difference being that the cost has gone up. They used to be content with an English sixpence; now they much prefer an American dollar.'

'And you?' She looked him straight in the eye.

' There are more Americans,' he said.

He had not yet told her the precise nature of his business in St Vincent and there was no reason why he should. He had come to look for one of his skippers; that was as much as she needed to know.

The harbour was full of shipping, boats of every description, and one of them was the *Charlotte Lucia*, which Max owned. If she was already on charter he would be plunged immediately into the business of setting things right. When they finally went ashore, however, he appeared to be in no great hurry.

'Would you like to meet the Andersons straight away,' he asked, ' or would you rather do some sight-seeing?   Aunt Carrie said something about it being necessary.'

'Max, you needn't feel *obliged* to entertain me!' She felt angered by his manner and, somehow, at a loss. 'If you have work to do I can easily take care of Robin—and myself.'

'There's not much I can do till the morning,' he told her.   'Even if I rounded up Wilson now in one of the wharf bars it would be impossible to find any labour till first light.   We must make do with that.' He glanced down at her.   'Now, what's the matter?'

'I was thinking about Robin's bedtime,' she explained.

'He's been asleep half the afternoon.'

'Yes, I know, but—'

'He'd never forgive us if we went for a jaunt without him.   We'll have a meal and get back to the schooner for eight o'clock,' he decided.   'Then you can salve your conscience by putting him to bed.'

She had wondered if they would sleep aboard the schooner or find somewhere ashore for the night, but apparently Max meant to come back to the *Carmelita*. It had been a new experience for her curling up on the bunk next to Robin's sea-cot while Barbie occupied the smaller cabin next door, but she had a strong sus-picion that they were occupying the ' skipper's berth ', which was Max's prerogative.   All his personal posses-sions had been scattered around when they had first come aboard, but they had disappeared by the time the deck hand had brought down her suitcase.

'We'll get a landau,' Max said.   'It's still warm enough.'

The hired vehicle was old and smelt musty inside, but with the hood down it was comfortable enough. Barbie, giggling a little, got in to sit with Robin on the back seat and Vanessa took her place on his other side.   Max sat facing them when he had issued his orders to the driver.   They looked like any other family going for a pleasant excursion to the hills in the cool of the evening.

The landau began to climb almost immediately, up and up by a twisting, narrow road behind the town until they came to a palm-fringed park surrounded by magnificent white houses set in carefully-maintained lawns. Enormous red hibiscus screened them from the public view and cascades of flowering creepers hung down from their surrounding walls almost to pavement level. They drove on, winding up the hill until they were three hundred feet above sea-level and could look down on the whole vast panorama of the harbour. It was magnificent. Vanessa drew in a deep breath of appreciation as Robin pointed out the schooner with some excitement.

' The *Carmelita*!' he cried. ' Way down there. Isn't she little, Vanessa?'

' You'll be sleeping aboard her to-night,' Max reminded him. ' She'll seem big enough then.'

They drove across the hills into the interior of the island, where it was very warm. Little villages appeared and disappeared, their shy inhabitants standing in narrow doorways to watch them pass. It was a primitive scene in many respects, but everywhere they went there was the impression of happiness. They had chased the sunset up to this high level and presently Max stopped the car to let them watch as the great yellow ball of light sank finally into the sea. All the sky and the harbour and the distant ocean took fire until the whole world seemed ablaze.

' I've never seen such vivid colours before,' Vanessa said. ' Every night it's the same, but up here there's a sort of magic.'

She paused, unable to find adequate words in which to express her feelings, and Max allowed her to sit and stare for several minutes before he decided that they must go.

' I thought you would appreciate it,' he said. ' When you climb high and look back across the Caribbean you might be in a different world. We used to climb behind the house at La Sola—'

It was his turn to pause, but she knew that he had

114

remembered the past with pleasure this time. His childhood had been a happy one, as had Alex's. How sad that a chance encounter, a whim of fate, had tarnished these memories.

She thought about Diane all the way back to Kingstown.

Robin was tired enough to curl up in his sea-cot as soon as they got back to the *Carmelita* and Vanessa took his supper in on a tray. The schooner rocked gently on the tide, for there was no wind, and very soon he was sound asleep.

'I'll watch beside him,' Barbie offered. 'You go on deck beside master.'

But Vanessa could not go immediately. She knew that Max was out there by the rail, smoking a leisurely cheroot in the bright tropical starlight, but he could so easily want to be alone. After an hour, however, she ventured towards the companionway to stand just inside the door listening to the myriad sounds of the harbour and soon her eyes became accustomed to the half-light, but Max was nowhere to be seen.

Supposing that he could have gone ashore again, she walked aft towards the poop deck where she had sat all afternoon with Barbie and Robin, finding it deserted. The tide ran along the schooner's hull and a shroud slapped idly against the mast above her head. There was a riding-light on the forward mast, like a low, bright star, nearer than all the rest.

'I hadn't thought of you as an astronomer,' Max observed, close at her elbow.

She turned, startled by his nearness.

'I thought you'd gone ashore,' she said. 'I'm sorry.'

'Sorry?' he echoed. 'For what? Coming to look at the stars?'

She turned her head away.

'It must seem like trespass. I had no idea this was your particular hideaway.'

'The whole ship is available to me,' he told her. 'I have no particular place.'

'But you must have been out here when I came,' she protested. 'With so many shadows I didn't see you.'

He laughed abruptly.

'Are you trying to explain me away, or just yourself?' he asked. 'I was sitting over there with my back to the hatch wondering what I should do with you to-morrow. I had it worked out that Ruby Anderson would take care of you while I went in search of Dan Wilson.'

'There must surely be plenty to do in a place like Kingstown.' She felt an encumbrance again, someone who had to be 'taken care of' like Robin and Barbie. 'I wouldn't mind seeing something of the town itself, so perhaps we could hire a taxi.'

'Is that what you would like?'

'It's a suggestion, and it would relieve you of the responsibility of looking after two women and a small boy.'

She regretted the barbed shaft as soon as she had uttered it, but nothing she said seemed to disturb this man, who was immune to sarcasm.

'My mother would expect me to entertain you,' he told her. 'It's the custom in these islands; the stranger in our midst is our great concern. I'll do my best to show you the town.'

'You have business to attend to,' she reminded him. Let me take Barbie and Robin. We won't go far.'

He gazed across the dark water of the harbour to where the white fortress stood above the town.

'We'll see,' he said.

Vanessa's hands fastened over the rail. She should go below now, she supposed, leaving him there to enjoy the solitude of his own domain, but the night and the stars trapped her by his side. She knew that she would not fall asleep for a very long time if she did return to the cabin and her restlessness might disturb Robin.

'Do you ever sleep on deck?' she asked involuntarily.

'Beneath the stars? Frequently, but not very often in harbour. Besides, I have the watch to-night.'

'Am I—making it difficult for you?'

'Not particularly. A watch is easy enough to keep once your eyes become accustomed to the shadows.'

She looked along the deck and over to the wharf where the lights were strung along the waterfront.

'I think I would have been a sailor if I'd been a boy,' she said.

'You hadn't a brother?'

She shook her head.

'No, there's just my sister and me, but she married and went to France. I missed her very much, especially after our father died and there was nobody. Sometimes I wish that I'd been part of a large family.'

She saw his lips tighten.

'It has its advantages,' he admitted, 'especially when you're young.'

Thoughts of Alex assailed her and of Diane, who was Alex's wife. Max leaned on the rail beside her, lighting another cheroot. A breeze crept in from the sea, disturbing the water beneath them and it seemed as if a strange, dark spell had been broken. Along the shore the waterfront came to life as dark figures moved against the lights and the sound of a guitar drifted towards them. Played softly at first, the oddly haunting melody rose to a crescendo at the end, the final chords swelling against the darkness.

'It's the mood of the Islands,' Max said. 'Softly seductive yet sometimes harsh to the point of violence. You'll come to understand it if you stay here long enough. In a few weeks' time, at La Sola, you'll take part in the Carnival, and that, too, can be a salutary experience. At La Sola it's the genuine thing, not an exhibition thought up for the tourist trade and certainly not the mild concoction of Limbo and a steel band which passes for entertainment in the average fashionable hotel.'

'I'm going to enjoy it,' she told him, listening to the distant music. 'It's inspired by the night, isn't it? By bright stars and dark water and a young moon showing above the palms.'

'You're the complete romantic,' he smiled, casting the butt of his cheroot over the rail. 'Let's hope the

Islands don't treat you harshly.'

'I can't imagine that,' she said, gazing into the night.

The unseen guitarist played on and, once or twice, when she recognised a melody, she sang the words under her breath, completely captivated by her surroundings. All her inhibitions had melted into the shadows behind her, and although she could not see Max clearly it seemed that he was no longer impatient, that he did not wholly resent her being there.

'Time to turn in,' he said, at last, peering at his watch. 'It's after midnight.'

'So late?' It was difficult to believe. 'Can I order you a nightcap?'

'It wouldn't have much effect.' He smiled down at her. 'The cook went ashore while you were putting Robin to bed, but I'll get you some cocoa, if you like.'

'I gather you don't drink cocoa.'

'Laced with rum, it might be just palatable!'

'I couldn't think of anything more revolting,' she declared. 'Which way to the galley?'

He led the way along the deck to the forward companionway and down to the galley where a hurricane lamp swung to and fro with the movement of the ship.

'Duck your head,' he advised.

The galley was small but spotlessly clean. Max would insist on that, she thought, following him down. It was also a fascinating place with its row of copper-bottomed pans swinging on their hooks and the stacked blue and white china gleaming behind the storm-guards.

'My mother's idea,' Max informed her, indicating the colourful china. 'She decided I was living rough.'

He boiled water on one of the calor-gas rings while she mixed the cocoa in the mugs he had produced. It was strong and dark and looked coarser than the refined powder out of a tin to which she was used.

'It's our own,' Max said. 'Cocoa in the raw. If you don't like it you can swill it away.'

It was good, with far more flavour than any ordinary brand. Vanessa cupped her hands round the blue and white mug, conscious of a sudden warmth in Max's

118

presence which she had never felt before. It may have been because he was more relaxed in these familiar surroundings, less likely to meet Alex and stumble upon the past.

He poured a measure of rum into her drink.

'Makes you sleep,' he said.

Vanessa took a sip of the odd concoction.

'It's horrible!' She made a wry face. 'Who invented it?'

'The original pirates, I expect.' He was laughing at her now quite frankly. 'You have to be chilled to the marrow to really appreciate it.'

'I can imagine!'

They carried their mugs back on deck, leaning on the rail to watch the phosphorescence shimmering on the water. It was brighter than Vanessa had ever seen, glowing like a fire in the darkness, an essential part of the night's magic. There was very little sound now; the guitar players had disappeared and the wharf was deserted save for a dark shape moving here and there among the shadows shuffling off towards the town where the lights were still shining, defying the stars with their artificial brilliance. The busy life of Kingstown seemed far removed from where they stood, with only a soft white blur in the background to show them Fort Charlotte, eternally watching.

Vanessa drank her nightcap slowly, prolonging the intimacy of the moment because it was the first time she had ever felt at peace with Max. She had recognised his strength and sense of purpose from the beginning, but this was something different.

'Are you up there, Skipper?'

A voice broke the spell and a man detached himself from the shadows on the wharf. She saw Max's frown as the light from the bulkhead behind them caught his face.

'Yes, what do you want?' he asked.

A black-visaged stranger put a foot on the gangplank.

'Come aboard,' Max said with reluctance.

Vanessa wondered if their visitor could be Wilson,

the man Max was looking for. Even in the half-light she could make out his small, shifty eyes and the coarse lips which were not quite hidden by the thick growth of black beard, and she drew back involuntarily.

'I'll go below,' she murmured.

Max passed her his empty beaker.

'Thank you,' he said without inviting her to stay.

His visitor shuffled along the deck, stepping to one side as she passed.

'Good-night, ma'am!' He doffed a greasy cap, but there was something insolent in the smile he offered.

'Good-night,' Vanessa murmured, glancing back at Max.

Something which might have been precious had been spoiled by the stranger's coming, something she might never recapture however hard she tried.

From the cabin she could hear their voices, their conversation going on far into the night.

Max made no reference to their sinister-looking visitor the following morning. He seemed to have forgotten him, although at times he seemed preoccupied.

'I've arranged for you to go across the island,' he informed her. 'I'll be in Georgetown most of the morning, but I'll join you for lunch.' He scribbled the name of a hotel on the card he tossed across the table. 'In case you forget,' he said.

Robin was frankly disappointed, but he accepted the fact that his uncle had to work occasionally.

'You can have fun on the beach with Barbie,' Max pointed out, 'and then we might go to see the Andersons.'

Vanessa was eager enough to explore the rest of the island which was dominated by its giant volcano, but when they drove in the taxi along the windward coast the beaches were black. Great rollers came pounding in from the Atlantic to wash across the lava sand, making bathing impossible, yet the coastal scenery was breathtaking.

Then, almost miraculously, the scene changed; they were over a long spur covered in a jungle growth of trees and bearing down on the gentle Caribbean once more. The taxi driver pulled into a white-sanded bay where they spent the remainder of the morning splashing about in the surf. It was almost one o'clock by the time Vanessa looked at her watch.

'Barbie!' she called. 'Quickly! We'll be late.'

The thought of Max cooling his heels at their rendezvous urged her on, but it was half-past one before they finally reached the hotel. Max was nowhere to be seen. He's gone off, she thought, in a rage, I wouldn't wonder, affronted at the idea of being kept waiting.

'I'm hungry,' Robin lamented.

'In a minute,' Vanessa promised, searching the foyer for the tall, familiar figure of his uncle. 'We're late, which is a very bad thing to be, and your uncle will have every reason to be vexed.'

'Will he be vexed with you?' Robin asked hopefully.

'Yes. You see I was in charge.'

'You could ask him to forgive you.'

She smiled.

'I may even have to do that.'

The foyer was emptying; people, having met, were making their way into the dining-room to claim their tables. Barbie seemed particularly interested in a group beside the door. It was quite a large party, obviously American, with one outstandingly beautiful girl who could have been any nationality. Even from across the foyer Vanessa could feel the strong pull of a vibrant personality, yet there was something instinctively sad about the other girl's face. Her eyes were enormously large and languid, her figure perfect, but she seemed to be taking very little interest in what was going on around her. The penetrating voices of the American women reached Vanessa across the foyer.

'Waal, I jus' don't see why not,' one of them argued. 'We've gotten here and it isn't far to the Grenadines. You said so, didn't you, Henry? You said it wasn't far to Grenada,' she repeated, nudging the portly figure by her side who had been in conversation with the lovely young woman.

'Oh, sure, sure!' Henry responded. 'One island is just like any other, I always say, but if you want to go to Grenada, you sure have to go, Laureen. We'll fix it. Yes, we'll sure fix that right away!'

They were obviously cruising among the Antilles and Vanessa could easily imagine the size and opulence of the yacht necessary to accommodate such a large party. It would be palatial and perhaps a little vulgar, not at all like the schooner with her lovely lines and tall twin masts lying down there in the harbour awaiting their return.

The hotel receptionist came towards them.

'Miss Gilbert?' he asked.

'Yes?' Vanessa looked anxious.

'I have a message for you from Mr Rossiter, ma'am. Will you be kind enough to take your lunch alone? Mr Rossiter has been delayed at Georgetown, but will pick you up at half-past two.'

'Oh—thank you!' It was absurd to feel such a rush of relief because Max needn't know how late she had been for their appointment. 'We'll go in straight away.'

They were escorted to a table at the edge of the covered patio overlooking the sea and Robin wriggled eagerly into a chair. Tiny birds fluttered above their heads, darting between the tables hoping to pick up a crumb or two.

'Can I have ice-cream first?' Robin wanted to know.

'You can have it for your dessert,' Vanessa answered firmly. 'Would you like some flying fish or snapper to start with? Barbie, what will you have?'

Barbie, who rarely dined out in such style, was too overcome to order for herself.

'Ah'll jus' take the same as Robin,' she decided. 'Ah mighty hungry, Miss Gilbert.'

Vanessa was aware of the American party occupying a large table in the centre of the room with half a dozen waiters hovering around them, anxious to please. The stout little man with the rasping voice was probably very wealthy indeed.

When their own meal was brought to the table they ate heartily and finally Robin was rewarded with a large goblet of coloured ice-cream.

'Uncle Max always lets me have one,' he announced, digging out spoonfuls of the luscious concoction.

Vanessa glanced at her watch. It was almost half-past two and she knew that Max would be punctual.

'We'll have to hurry,' she warned. 'Eat up the rest of your ice quickly, Robbie, and we'll look for your uncle.'

Max was striding across the foyer as they went out through the swing doors. He was obviously well known at the hotel and had already paid their bill. Vanessa saw him coming towards them with a little glow of pride in her heart, realising how good it was to be looked after in this way.

Before he reached them, however, Max hesitated, drawn up sharply as his gaze went beyond them to the room they had just left. The colour went completely out of his face and a pulse beat suddenly at his temple.

'We had a lovely lunch,' Robin informed him, tugging at his hand, but he did not seem to hear.

'I have a car waiting,' he said automatically, his gaze still riveted on the open patio they had just left. 'We have to clear harbour by five o'clock.'

His brows were drawn in a deep frown as he hustled them through the main doorway into the waiting car and Vanessa was left to wonder what he had seen in the restaurant to shatter his habitual composure.

They drove directly to the harbour, boarding the schooner with the crew, who had been out 'on the town' for the morning. Max gave his orders as they made their way down to the cabin.

'We'll sail immediately.'

He seemed determined not to linger in Kingstown for a moment longer than he could help and Vanessa knew a sense of deepest relief when they were finally heading out of the bay.

As they rounded Young's Island the sun plunged down into the Caribbean, staining its blue to gold and then crimson. Little ripples of golden cloud sailed above the horizon with streaks of apricot light fanning up behind them and over everything the silence of deep water dropped like balm. The schooner's bows cleft the waves with a sharp hissing sound, but that was all. In this vast expanse of crimson sea they were the only ship in sight, a fact which lent a solitude to their journey which was true enchantment.

Protesting sleepily, Robin was finally put to bed.

'You go on deck, Missie Gilbert,' Barbie advised. 'I stay here an' watch all the time.'

She had curled up outside the cabin door, proud of her new importance, and Vanessa decided to take her advice. The deck was deserted, but she had not come in search of Max. Not consciously. To be out in the open under those incredible stars with the cool trade wind blowing the hair back from her forehead and the sound of the waves in her ears was enough. She leaned against the rail watching the white bow-wave curl up and lose itself in the dark water, and suddenly Max seemed very near.

Turning swiftly, she sought his approach along the deck, but the whole ship seemed to be deserted. To imagine him near must have been a trick of her imagination simply because the sea was his natural element and she had been made aware of its fascination for the first time.

A buccaneer! The word seemed to be wafted to her on the night wind. A pirate by name and by nature. She laughed the thought aside.

'What amuses you so much?' He had come up behind her out of the shadows lurking beneath the shrouds. 'I thought you might be tired after your long morning on the beach.'

'It was a lazy morning swimming and lying on the sand. We were late getting to the hotel.' Suddenly nothing but the truth seemed possible between them. 'In a way I was glad you hadn't been waiting for half an hour.'

She turned towards him, only half aware of him, even now. The colour had gone from the sky, leaving a pearl-grey band along the horizon. Suddenly she was in his arms.

' Max—'

The hard pressure of his lips silenced her as her thoughts dissolved around her. Only the grip of his hands on her bare shoulders was real as she stood there, accepting his kiss, desiring it, yet shattered by its harsh intensity until, equally abruptly, he let her go.

' So much for the night and the stars!' he said grimly. ' Do you want me to apologise?'

' Not unless you're sorry.' She hardly recognised her own voice.

He laughed.

' Should I be?'

' I don't know.'

' You could answer me one question.

' Yes?'

' Do you belong to Alex?'

' I'm here to work for him.'

' That's no kind of answer. Are you in love with him?'

' I don't think so.'

' Either you know or you don't.' He turned from her with a show of impatience. ' But we won't argue the point.'

' Max—'

He lit a cheroot, the flame from the match flaring in his eyes for a second before it was extinguished.

' I'll take you below,' he said. ' The wind has turned cold.'

The indifference in his voice chilled her more than any wind could have done and she could not protest against his decision. He stood at the head of the companionway until she had reached the cabin and then he turned back along the deck. To-morrow, she thought, he will have forgotten all this, but she would never forget. Even as she walked away from him, his savage kiss still seared her lips and she knew that she would live with the memory of it in her heart for the rest of her life.

CHAPTER VI

Alex was at the bay to meet them. He had come in with the freighter an hour before and was standing on the stone jetty as the schooner made her way gracefully towards it. There was undisguised fury in his eyes as he greeted them.

'Where have you been?' he demanded. 'Don't tell me Max has taken to cruising round the lagoon for want of something better to do.'

'We went to Kingstown,' Vanessa explained. 'It was to please Robin, and your mother had Aunt Carrie and the doctor to keep her company.'

'To please Robin?' he echoed. 'Don't give me that. Why not be honest and say it was to please yourself and Max?'

'You can't really believe that Max *wanted* to take me,' Vanessa protested, 'but he had promised Robin, and your mother thought it would be a chance for me to see the Islands.'

'Admirable, I'm sure.' He seemed less angry as Robin and Barbie came towards them. 'My mother's a great organiser. I hope Carrie hasn't upset her.'

'Is she likely to?' Vanessa seized on the less personal issue. 'I thought they got on very well together.'

'They do, more or less, but that was no excuse for you deserting your post.'

'I'm sorry.' She always seemed to be apologising to Alex. 'I'll make up for my little jaunt by working all day to-morrow, I promise you.'

It was a promise she was determined to keep, although she was well ahead with the chapter Alex had asked her to finish. Robin had claimed his father's attention and they walked up the dust road to La Sola without waiting for Max, who did not seem to be in any hurry to join them. Looking at her employer closely for the first time, Vanessa imagined that Alex was slightly preoccupied, but once they had reached the house he appeared to be his old, charming self. Carrie Hazeltine was greatly amused by him, rising to the challenge of his remarks with gusto, and the doctor, who was never averse to young company, departed for the bay where he would board the freighter with reluctance.

Max failed to put in an appearance until after the evening meal, going along the corridor to his den almost immediately.

' I suppose he's being boot-faced about the library,' Alex observed, ' but he can't just lay claim to the whole house because he happened to stay put when I went away.' He got up to prowl around the room, suddenly restless as he contemplated the night sky above the lagoon. ' I'm going out,' he announced. ' I'll see you in the morning, Vanessa, bright and early. It's high time we did some work.'

' I should never have gone to St Vincent,' Vanessa said, sitting in the chair beside Helena. ' I knew I had work to do and I should have finished it. After all, I came here as Alex's secretary.'

Helena sighed.

' Max was angry to-night, and Alex's attitude doesn't help,' she admitted. ' I feel greatly saddened by the antagonism between my two sons.'

' Was I the cause of it to-night?' Vanessa asked.

Helena shook her head.

' You know it goes deeper than that.'

Carrie rose from her chair.

' Max should have got over Diane by now,' she declared. ' He's not the sort to break his heart over a woman who played him false years ago.'

' How can we tell?' Helena said. ' Max would never let anyone see into his heart. Not now.'

Vanessa rose unsteadily to her feet. Was she always to be reminded of Diane in connection with Max, she wondered, or would the memory of that savage kiss recede in time and leave her free?

' You look tired,' Helena said. ' It's time we were all in bed.'

It was an hour later before Alex returned. Vanessa heard his footsteps on the verandah and the careless slam of a door as he went to his own room. There was no sign of Max, but it would have been easy for him to go out into the night again without walking through the house, coming and going by the side entrance as he pleased.

She did not see him again for over a week. The harvesters arrived from Grenada the following morning, filling the valley with noisy activity as they cut their way into the cane, slicing great swathes through it with their deadly-looking machetes to open out a path for the machines. Much of the preliminary work was done by hand, the men singing as they reaped, the women gleaning after them.

Vanessa knew that Max was down there in the cane fields with the labour force, working as hard as any of them, because the schooner still lay at anchor in the bay and a lamp burned in the window of his room far into the night. He seemed to need very little sleep, since he was up again by five in the morning before any of them were awake and only returned when the light had faded.

Vanessa spent most of her time at her typewriter, almost despairing of pleasing her employer now. Alex seemed tensed and unable to concentrate, breaking off periodically in mid-sentence, which suggested that his mind was not on his work. When he was dictating he prowled about the library, picking up books here and there only to lay them down again and begin anew, scrubbing out much which she had already typed. The final chapters of his book were going to be difficult.

' I'm going to lay off for a while to-morrow,' he intimated at the end of the week. ' I'm going fishing.'

' Do you want me to type this chapter again?' Vanessa asked.

' If you like, but I warn you I could easily change it.' He ran his fingers through his hair. ' I can't seem to concentrate. Maybe it was the wrong thing to do, coming here.'

' I don't think so,' Vanessa said. ' You've made such a friend of Robin.'

It was true. Robin had now accepted him without reservation, although he had not quite transferred the whole of his allegiance from Max. There was something exciting about having two grown men in the family and having Tom's return to look forward to into the bargain.

'Where will you go?' Vanessa asked.

'I'll take the schooner.' Alex looked round at her. 'Why not? Max won't be using it for another week, at least.'

She presumed that he would ask his brother's permission and was pleased when he said he was taking Robin with him.

'Time he learned to fish properly,' he decided.

He could afford to leave his book for a while, Vanessa thought, especially to cultivate his son's acquaintance. Helena also seemed pleased with the arrangement.

'You can go down and watch the cane being cut,' she told Vanessa.

'Do you think Max would mind?' Vanessa wondered.

'Mind? Why should he? Besides, he'll likely be far too busy to notice you. Keep away from the machines—and watch out for the machetes. The boys wield them with vicious force,' Helena warned.

Vanessa was determined not to go to the valley until the work Alex had left her to do was on his desk, and with that end in view she worked all the following morning typing at speed. Then and only then would she go down to the cane fields, waiting till the workers had completed their siesta. The heat of the sun at midday was beginning to affect her now and she often rested on her verandah after her light lunch, but today she decided to work on.

Over the sound of the typewriter she heard Max's voice.

'My mother said you would like to come down to the fields,' he said, coming further into the room. 'Bring a hat with you. It's more than a little warm down there just now.'

His sudden appearance had startled her, but she sought for composure to answer him.

' I hope you don't mind my coming. I know how busy you are down there just now.'

' Come, by all means,' he said. ' The overseer will show you round.'

She fought with her disappointment, calling it childish.

' Is the cutting finished?'

' Not quite. We have a fair spread of cane right up the valley. You may like to go up in the truck if they're loading.'

He was entirely dissociating himself with her visit, but she was still determined to go.

' For my education's sake I think I ought to see cane being cut!' she told him.

Already, all over La Sola, they were aware of it. The sound of men's voices came in to them through the open windows and the sweet, cloying scent of the cut sugar was strong in the air. Wafted towards the lagoon on the breath of the wind, it drifted far out to sea, mingling with the scent of pineapple and the smell of burning wood.

Max walked to the edge of the verandah to look down towards the lagoon. A yacht had come in over the reef at high tide and was anchored at the leeward side of the Bluff. Vanessa got up from her machine to look at it.

' Are they safe?' she asked.

' If they remember about the tide.' He was frowning. ' We get very few visitors here.'

A launch pulled away from the yacht's side, streaking across the lagoon to the small wooden jetty down on the shore, and the sound of its engine was suddenly raucous in the silence.

' I wonder who they are,' Max said.

He continued to watch their unexpected visitors' progress as they left the launch and filed up the beach. There were four of them, two men and two women, and something about them was suddenly curiously familiar to Vanessa. She caught her breath, recognising the party of Americans from the hotel on St Vincent. There could be no mistaking the graceful figure of the girl she had admired so much nor the paunchy little man nor, in fact, the older woman with the raucous voice. They were advancing on La Sola as if they had every right to be there.

Swiftly Vanessa turned towards her companion.

'They were in the hotel at Kingstown,' she offered before she became fully aware of the look on Max's face.

'And now they're here.' His eyes were the mirrors of a dark and satanic passion as he strode past her. 'Perhaps you'll go to my mother. This is going to be a shock to her.'

Vanessa's heart seemed to jump straight into her throat as the little group came steadily on. She had been right when she had recognised them as the people from the hotel on St Vincent, but it was the younger woman who led them now. She walked straight to the foot of the verandah where Helena was seated with her embroidery on her knee enjoying the end of her afternoon's rest.

Vanessa walked forward under the pergola where a little yellow bird was chirping. She could see Helena's face now and it was also mask-like, except for the eyes, which held the shadow of defeat.

'Hullo, Helena!' the girl said. 'Don't tell me you're surprised to see me!'

Without having to be told, Vanessa knew that this was Diane.

Alex's wife! For a moment she refused to believe it, and then there could be no mistaking the beauty and assurance of the girl she had only heard about until now.

'Surely you knew I would come back,' Diane said in her silky voice.

'You took your time.' Helena was struggling with anger and near-despair. 'Why have you come, Diane? What do you want?'

'I want my son.'

In spite of her show of confidence, Diane was nervous, and even with her friends from the yacht to back her up she was afraid of Helena. For a fleeting moment she looked beyond her mother-in-law to where Max stood.

'If you don't mean to stay here,' Helena said, 'you'll only be upsetting Robin.'

Diane looked about her.

'I'm older now,' she said. 'It could make a difference.'

'What sort of answer is that?' Helena demanded. 'You haven't changed. You still like the gay life, by the looks of things—yachts and parties and the like. You would never settle here. It would be the same mischief all over again, the same heartbreak and futile wrangling, and this time Robin would be deeply involved. When you left he was no more than a baby; he didn't even know you, but now—now if he met you he would understand.'

'*If* he met me?' Diane queried, glancing across the lawn to where her companions were admiring the garden. 'What do you mean?'

Helena hesitated, looking for Max, who had gone to intercept the Americans.

'Alex has taken him on a fishing trip.'

'Alex!' Diane swung round to look at Vanessa for the first time. 'I see,' she said carefully. 'And what does Alex think about me coming back to La Sola?'

Helena's lips firmed.

'He'll have to answer that question for himself.' She turned to Vanessa. 'This is Alex's wife, my dear,' she explained. 'Perhaps we had better ask—our visitors to stay for tea.'

Diane sat down on one of the long cane chairs.

'Everything is just the same,' she remarked, flinging aside her brightly-coloured headscarf. 'La Sola never changes, does it? But people do,' she added quickly. 'Max has changed out of all proportion, I would say. We've heard about him up and down the Islands— how successful he is and how mysterious.' She laughed a little. 'I used to feel sorry for Max,' she confessed, 'but not now. He's quite—mature, wouldn't you say?'

Whatever Helena had thought of saying was interrupted by Max as he brought the remainder of the yachting party to the foot of the verandah steps.

'I'd like you to meet my friends, the Schoebergs,' Diane said, leaning forward in her chair. 'And this is Ava Perani. We're all on Carlo's yacht, but he has stayed behind this afternoon to do something to the engines. Or maybe he's just fishing!' she laughed, her dark eyes lighting up as they rested on Carlo Perani's wife. 'Ava calls herself a golf widow, but I think she ought to go into the question of fish!'

The big American woman laughed heartily, coming heavily up the verandah steps to shake hands.

'Now, don't you get up,' she remonstrated to Helena. 'I can see you were resting, and maybe that's what I should have been doing as well in all this heat, but Diane here wanted so much for us to come ashore with her that it would have seemed downright churlish to refuse. She's told us a whole lot about you, Mrs Rossiter, and about La Sola.' She gazed across the garden and the banana plantation to the still water of the lagoon. 'It sure is a lovely place, as she said.'

Helena's eyebrows shot up; she was obviously sceptical of Diane's admiration for her former home.

Vanessa hurried into the kitchens to order tea. The screens had been closed against the midday sun and the house felt cold rather than cool.

'We'll have the jalousies back, Teresa,' she suggested when the coloured girl came hurrying towards her, 'and then you can bring tea to the verandah. Mrs Rossiter has unexpected guests.'

'Yeah, sure, Miss Gilbert, ma'am.' Teresa was still shy in Vanessa's presence. 'I see them come up from the beach an' I say to myself that done sure look like Mister Alex's woman.'

Vanessa bit her lip; she was not quite sure just how much the servants knew.

'Make plenty of tea,' she directed. 'There are eight of us.'

Wondering if she should have included Max in their

number, she made her way back to the verandah to find him still there talking with Henry Schoeberg about boats. Diane had settled back in her chair, listening to the conversation between Mrs Schoeberg and Carrie, who had joined the tea party, and Helena also listened, although her eyes were on her son.

It was difficult to gauge Max's reaction to this meeting with the girl he had once loved, and Diane seemed slightly piqued by his lack of interest. Once she had been the desirable woman—desirable to two men—and now she had met Max again and he was seemingly quite content to ignore her while he discussed yachts with Henry Schoeberg. Playing second fiddle was a position in which Diane rarely found herself, especially second fiddle to a boat.

The Americans proved to be lively company. They had come through the Canal from Acapulco de Juárez and had sailed all over the Caribbean. It had taken them three months, but they were still avid for further adventure. The yacht was a charter and it had given them trouble at times, and Vanessa heard Henry Schoeberg asking if Max would accommodate him the following year.

'Nothing like knowing who you're dealing with!' he boomed. 'I'd need a biggish job, you understand, and an experienced skipper to go with her. I fish a lot.'

Max promised to supply him with the relevant details.

'You wouldn't think of coming along yourself?' Schoeberg asked in his blunt manner. 'I feel we'd get on together.'

Diane held her breath, waiting for Max's answer.

'I rarely go out with a charter,' he said firmly, 'but I have three competent skippers I can call on when they are wanted. Two, at least, I can thoroughly recommend.'

Henry Schoeberg thought that would be good enough.

'At my age you have to get away now and then,' he confided. 'We're from Pittsburgh. Made my money in steel, as a matter of fact.' He lit a cigar. 'I see you're in sugar and cocoa. Does it pay its way?'

Max seemed highly amused by his frankness, but Helena was showing signs of restlessness. Their visitors from the yacht were clearly overstaying their welcome as far as she was concerned. Diane, however, was evidently determined to wait until Alex got back.

They saw the schooner rounding the headland on the far side of the lagoon, but Alex carried on to the bay to drop anchor. It would be some time before he made his appearance at La Sola. Diane turned her attention to Vanessa.

'Are you here on holiday, Miss Gilbert?' she asked.

'Oh, no, I'm strictly on a working trip,' Vanessa answered. 'I'm typing Alex's latest book.'

Diane looked interested.

'He's done quite well, I understand.' She was still searching Vanessa's face. 'He always said he would. Trouble was, he wanted to do it here.'

'I can imagine,' said Vanessa. 'La Sola is the ideal spot for a writer, there's so much peace.'

'Is that what they need?' The dark eyes were inscrutable. 'Alex seemed to thrive on controversy at one time. He used to say that it kept him alert. I'm going to find him changed.'

The atmosphere had become charged with an odd sense of conflict; they all seemed to be playing some fantastic game in which no one was able to trust the other. In a moment or two Helena would be forced to order drinks and ask her visitors to stay. She glanced anxiously towards the Bluff.

When the two expected figures made their appearance at the head of the path Diane rose to her feet. She stood at the edge of the verandah, her eyes on the pathway through the garden, her lips parted a little to show her excellent teeth, and it seemed as if she held her breath until her son and her husband were near enough to recognise.

There was a movement at the back of the verandah and Vanessa turned to see Max striding off in the direction of the cane fields. He had excused himself to his guests and was making his escape now that Alex

135

had come back.

Vanessa's throat felt suddenly dry. It had been his first opportunity to leave them and he had taken it as quickly as possible. She watched his tall figure disappearing among the cane, trying not to remember how he had kissed her so short a time ago, trying not to think that there might have been something in the night which had reminded him of Diane.

Alex did not seem to be greatly surprised when he saw his wife. Still holding Robin by the hand, he looked Diane straight in the eye.

'I heard you were somewhere around,' he said. 'In Bridgetown, as a matter of fact.'

Perhaps that was what had taken him to Barbados so urgently on receipt of the mysterious letter, Vanessa thought. Diane looked beyond him to Robin, all the bright colour fading from her cheeks.

'Hullo, darling!' she greeted him. 'Haven't you got a loving kiss for your mother?'

The Schoebergs moved to go.

'We'll pick you up with the launch later on, Diane,' they offered. 'Right now, I think we ought to make our way back to the yacht.'

Diane seemed hardly aware of them. She was holding out her arms to Robin, who came towards her reluctantly.

'You can't expect the child to remember you, Alex said harshly.

'Give him time.' Diane was smiling at her son. 'He's grown so big! Did you catch all these fish by yourself, Robin?' she asked. 'They're almost too heavy to hold.'

Vanessa went with the Schoebergs to see them safely to the beach, too shaken to take much part in their conversation but well aware of Mrs Schoeberg's curiosity.

'It's a funny situation,' that lady commented. 'Diane and her husband, I mean. Do you think they'll ever get to being together again, Miss Gilbert?'

'I don't know them well enough to answer that.' Vanessa had never felt so confused. 'I only work for

Mr Rossiter.'

'We met Diane through a mutual friend,' Laureen Schoeberg explained, 'and Carlo and Ava asked her to come along on this trip with us because she seemed so—what's the word I want? Lost, maybe. She just seemed to be wandering aimlessly from one party to the next in Acapulco, not really enjoying any of them. If you ask me, she hasn't made the success of her career she hoped for and she's disillusioned. There are hundreds like her; they see the glamour and excitement of acting while they choose to ignore the facts.'

'If you ask me,' Ava Perani said, 'Diane wouldn't ignore anything. She's far too smart for that. She must have weighed it all up and discovered that it wasn't what she wanted, after all.'

'If she wants something here,' Laureen mused, 'she won't get it without a tussle. Not this time. And if she's playing games she might be sorry.'

'I guess so,' Ava agreed.

Henry Schoeberg took off his peaked sun-cap to scratch his head.

'I dunno,' he said. 'She struck me as real genuine.'

His wife gave him a pitying look.

'So she would, Henry,' she acknowledged dryly. 'She's a woman and a pretty one at that, but I still say she could be real mean if the spirit moved her.'

'She seemed real fond of the little boy,' Henry murmured.

'She's his mother,' Laureen, who was childless, said curtly.

They had reached the beach where the white launch from the yacht was waiting for them.

'How long will you be staying?' Vanessa heard herself asking the conventional question while she recognised, deep in her heart, how personal it really was.

'A day or two; maybe not that,' Mrs Perani answered. 'It will depend on the fishing, I guess. Carlo likes a safe anchorage for the yacht and there's lots of scope for fishing around the lagoon, apparently. Yes,' she decided, 'we could be here for a day or two.'

They got into the launch and Vanessa stood on the

beach until it was half-way across the lagoon. It would return to pick up Diane, or perhaps she would send word across to the yacht that she was staying at La Sola overnight.

Reluctantly she retraced her footsteps through the bananas towards the house. The sun was well down on the horizon and soon it would be dark, that swift darkness which could still surprise her. In the shade of the bananas deep shadows were already spread across her path and when she reached the garden the verandah was deserted. Or it seemed deserted until she was near enough to see the slight figure standing in the shadows. It was Diane.

A movement at the foot of the verandah told her that Diane was not alone. A man was seated on the steps, hunched forward with his hands clasped between his knees, staring at the ground. Vanessa froze where she stood because it was impossible to go on and almost as impossible to retreat without being detected. Her heart began to pound in her breast like a caged animal.

'I've seen Robin now.' Diane's voice came out of the shadows like some haunted thing. 'I've seen him and I know what I want.'

'It's out of the question.' Alex's voice was tense with suppressed emotion. 'You can't just walk out and stay away for three years, then come back and *claim* him.'

'Why not? I'm his mother, remember.' There was anger in Diane's voice now. 'He's mine!'

'Why this sudden interest?' Alex got slowly to his feet. 'You haven't bothered about him for three whole years.'

'I need him.' Diane moved forward into the dying light. 'I need something in my life to act as a sheet anchor.'

Alex looked savage.

'If you can't give me a better reason than that,' he said, 'my answer is "no".'

'We're not divorced!' Diane cried. 'I have a right to see my child.'

'Which you sacrificed long ago,' he pointed out

138

acidly.

There was a long pause in which Vanessa looked around her for a possible way of escape. She did not want to be seen, but she shrank from eavesdropping further in this argument between husband and wife. At any moment now her own name might be mentioned, she thought, remembering how Diane had looked at her, and she did not want Alex to say they were in love to spite his errant wife.

' Was that your only reason for coming here?' She heard his voice, coldly accusing, from the verandah steps.

' Not altogether.' Diane sounded curiously shaken.

' Give me another reason,' Alex demanded.

' Perhaps I'm tired of gadding about the world.'

' Don't tell me that!'

' You wouldn't believe me if I did. I know that. You never credited me with any decent feelings, did you, Alex?'

' You hardly gave me cause.'

' You're bitter.' Diane's voice had softened. ' Why? Are you in love with the peaches-and-cream English girl—your secretary?'

' I could be. Three years is a long time, Diane.'

' You've done your own share of roving,' she reminded him.

' To a purpose.'

' I've heard about your success, of course.'

Alex's harsh laughter disturbed the night.

' Is that what brings you back?' he demanded. ' Comparative wealth?'

' No— that wasn't why.' The fire had gone out of Diane now. ' Where is Max?' she asked.

' Here somewhere, but I've half a notion he's got over you, Diane,' Alex said grimly. ' If he hasn't, don't expect him to rush with open arms to meet you. You were in love with him once—'

He stood waiting. What did he want her to say? Deny it?

' I saw him in Kingstown,' Diane admitted, ' but he was boarding the schooner and it was too late to contact him. He was with your secretary.'

Vanessa moved backwards along the shrubbery path, the deepening shadows obscuring her, at last. She could go down through the plantation again and round the house to the side door, to Max's secret entrance which nobody used but himself.

Going past the nursery she heard Robin protesting to Barbie,

' I don't want to go to bed. I want to stay up and see my mother.'

Barbie, who had ' mothered ' him for the past two years under Helena's strict supervision, felt herself discredited.

' Shoo, you don' want to go hollerin' for you mammy like a great baby! ' she admonished. ' You big now, like a grown man. Like you Uncle Max,' she added thoughtfully.

Vanessa hurried along the corridor, her eyes suddenly full of the tears she could not shed.

Helena had joined her son and daughter-in-law on the verandah and Carrie followed Vanessa from the drawing-room. Max was nowhere to be seen, yet his den had been empty, the door flung wide, the jalousies still closed, which suggested that he had not been there all afternoon.

Alex was pouring drinks at the table.

' Something with lime in it, Vanessa?' he asked as she stepped into the light.

' Thank you.'

His hand shook as he passed her the tall glass and she noticed that he poured himself a neat rum. Diane asked for pineapple juice.

' How long are you staying, Diane?' Carrie broke the awkward silence between them.

' I'm not sure.' Diane was really uncertain now. ' I suppose as long as Carlo Perani wants to fish from the lagoon.'

' And then?'

Diane hesitated.

' I may go as far as Barbados,' she said.

Vanessa wondered about Max. It was almost dark

now, the sun gone down into a grey sea with no glory in its setting, and the workers long since returned from the cane fields. Already the sound of their singing could be heard from their encampment farther up the valley and the glow of their wood fires illumined the distant trees. The young ones would sing and dance far into the night, yet they would not fail to turn up for work in the morning. It was their way of life.

Diane heaved a deep sigh.

'I must go,' she said. 'Fishermen like to get early to bed!'

Perhaps the sea trip was already boring her; perhaps she had expected more of her little adventure as a guest aboard the chartered yacht.

Alex rose to accompany her to the beach.

'Coming?' he asked Vanessa.

'I—have a few things I must do before dinner,' Vanessa answered hastily, aware that he had been willing to use her as a barrier between himself and his wife, the third party who would make further recrimination impossible until Diane boarded the launch and streaked away across the lagoon.

Dinner proved to be a difficult meal because everyone was far too preoccupied with their own thoughts to make easy conversation. Max did not put in an appearance and Alex was restless, prowling along the verandah afterwards with a cheroot between his lips which finally went out. He flung it from him into the garden.

'Why the devil had she to come here?' he demanded of the night in general. 'She wouldn't have stayed, even if I had agreed.'

'Did she ask to stay?' Helena wanted to know.

'Not in so many words.'

Vanessa turned away, excusing herself. This was a family matter.

It was not quite ten o'clock and she could put in an hour's work on Alex's book. The library was empty and she wondered if she had been foolish enough to hope that she might find Max there.

Alex's new masterpiece was so compelling that it kept her enthralled till midnight. She had been completely carried away by the story, even though she was typing it and correcting as she went along. In this respect, at least, Alex had come to rely on her, she mused, pushing back her chair to massage the tightened muscles at the nape of her neck.

The windows leading on to the verandah were wide open and a dozen tiny moths strayed in from the garden, encircling the desk lamp and she switched it off, standing for a moment in the darkness till the glittering stars above the cequita palms shed a softer radiance on the world outside. There had been a sharp, heavy shower of rain less than an hour before, leaving great drops of moisture on the shining leaves of the hibiscus and bright little puddles on the terrace steps. It had washed the garden clean and the banana fronds were still heavy under its weight, the air still cool. It had silenced the guitars in the valley encampment and dimmed the glow-worm light of the distant fires, but she was still conscious of the murmur which came from a throng of happy people settling down for the night. When the cane was fully gathered in they would take time off to play and she would witness the full meaning of carnival. Max had promised her that, yet this day's events could easily cancel out all thoughts of rejoicing within the family at La Sola.

She stood there, thinking about Diane and wondering about Max and Alex till a movement in the garden beneath her made her catch her breath. There was very little need for alarm at La Sola because strangers rarely came that way, but suddenly her heart was pounding and she was stepping back into the shadows in an effort at concealment.

A man walked towards her. He was tall and very thin, made slimmer in the starlight by the fact that he had been soaked through and his light clothes were clinging to his body like a second skin. His hair, plastered to his head, was black and shining, but it failed to conceal the scowl which disfigured his brows. For a moment she could not believe that this was really

Max.

Before she could retreat into the room itself he had seen her.

'What are you doing, up at this time of night?' he demanded.

'I was working.' Her voice shook a little.

'Working?' he repeated, his dark gaze going beyond her. 'Alex must be mad!'

'He probably hasn't any idea. He—went to see Diane to the launch and then he must have gone to bed. If he saw the light in the library he may have thought someone was looking for a book.' She stepped towards him. 'Your clothes are soaking,' she said with some concern. 'Let me get you a hot drink while you change them.'

He looked as if he would refuse her generous offer out of hand, his brows still darkly drawn together.

'Please,' she begged. 'You'll only catch a chill.'

He laughed the idea to scorn.

'If I'd caught a chill each time I've been soaked to the skin I wouldn't be here by now,' he informed her, 'but I will have that drink if you can rustle it up.' He peeled off his thin poplin jacket. 'I was caught on the mountain,' he explained. 'High up. There's absolutely no shelter once you've left the trees behind.'

He must have climbed over a thousand feet to have left the scrub behind, probably more, since he had been unable to reach any kind of shelter until he was soaked through. There didn't seem to be any reason why he should have gone up there, unless it had been to escape from his own thoughts and the presence of the woman he had once loved. If he was still in love with Diane, if he still wanted her, he would have fought his own personal battle up there on the cold slopes of the volcano.

She looked out at the mountain faintly etched against the star-bright sky.

'Wasn't it a dangerous thing to do in the dark?' she asked.

'Dangerous for anyone who doesn't know the mountain,' he agreed, 'but not for me. I've climbed it since

143

I was a schoolboy. Don't fear for me, Vanessa. The hounds of doubt may have been my fiendish companions, but I had them well in hand.'

'Don't talk in riddles,' she said more sharply than she realised, ' and go and have a shower. I'll see what I can do in the kitchens.'

When she came back with the hot drink she had prepared in the deserted kitchens he was waiting in the library, changed out of his wet clothes and wrapped in a printed dressing gown with the cord tied tightly about his waist. The savage look had left his face, although his eyes were still fierce.

'Did you take a shower?' she asked.

'I did.' He picked up one of the beakers from the tray she had set down on the desk. 'What awful concoction is this?'

'It's no worse than the rum drink you forced on me in the schooner,' she told him, trying to sound assertive. ' It's something my mother used to give us when we came in cold in the winter.'

He sampled it without enthusiasm.

'Nothing to beat rum,' he muttered aggressively.

'Where did you put your wet clothes?'

He turned to smile at her.

'Don't mother me, Vanessa. I'm not Robin,' he said.

'You're equally unconcerned about your safety. Robin is determined to climb the mountain,' she told him.

His eyes sharpened.

'See that he doesn't,' he warned briefly. ' It's no place for a child on his own.'

'I understand you promised to take him one day.'

'One day.' His mind was obviously on something else. 'What did you think of Diane?'

It was the question she had least expected.

'Diane?' she repeated foolishly. ' I thought she was —very beautiful.'

'I didn't expect you to be evasive.'

'Well then, I thought she was genuinely concerned about Robin.'

He frowned.

'Would you come back, under the circumstances?' he asked.

'If I thought my son needed me.'

He sipped his drink.

'Did my mother go to bed immediately?' The question dismissed Diane from their conversation.

'She went after dinner. I think she was very tired.'

'If you mean "upset", Vanessa, why don't you say so?'

'Sometimes it can be the same thing.'

'Yes,' he agreed, the frown back between his brows. 'But she had Carrie—and you.' He rose to replace the empty beaker. 'Thank heaven for that, at least.'

Vanessa moved towards the door.

'You won't go out again?' she appealed.

He came across the room, standing at the door to look down at her.

'No,' he said, 'I won't go out. I've climbed the mountain and made my decision.'

CHAPTER VII

The early morning sun had dried the sugar by the time
the first of the labourers reached the cane fields and
all morning long the loaded trucks trundled down the
valley and over the dirt road to the collecting sheds.
La Sola wasn't big enough to support its own crushing
plant and the cane was stacked under cover until it
could be shipped out to Grenada or one of the larger
islands.

Max and the foreman worked with the cutters, super-
vising and directing as the deep swathes were cut
through the cane. Every now and then there was some
crisis or another which called for their personal supervision, but generally the vast job of harvesting went on
to the accompaniment of laughter and song. When
the cutters laid aside their wicked-looking machetes
and sat down among the discarded stalks to rest and
quench their thirst someone inevitably produced a
guitar and the valley reverberated to a Caribbean love
song or the increasing tempo of Limbo.

Vanessa heard it as she worked with Alex in the
library. He had come in earlier than usual and was
surprised to see her already at her typewriter.

' You shame me,' he said, ' but I work better later in
the day.' He read over the first few sentences on the
quarto sheet she had rolled into the machine. ' What
do you think of it?'

' It's very good.' She was being completely honest.
' Are you going to do any more revision?'

He shook his head.

' We'll finish it now. I'm glad I had got this far
before I started to think about—other things.'

She knew that he meant Diane's unexpected appearance at La Sola, but she remained silent.

' Fact is,' he added, ' I ought to get away.'

She sat back in her seat to look at him.

' Leave La Sola?'

' Would that be so dreadful?' He took a quick turn

about the room. 'You haven't been here long enough to fall in love with a way of life.'

'Time doesn't come into it,' she said. I think I fell in love with La Sola as soon as I saw it.'

'Diane said much the same thing when Max first brought her here.' His voice was sharp with bitterness. 'She didn't mean it, of course.'

'There's just the possibility she might mean it now,' Vanessa suggested.

He smiled.

'Not Diane! She's too fond of the bright lights.'

She supposed he knew his wife better than anyone else and let the matter rest there.

Alex worked with a sort of fury after that, as if he had to prove something to someone.

'I've got to get this thing finished,' he said. 'I owe it to myself.'

In this frame of mind it was difficult to keep up with him. Vanessa spent all day typing until her fingers were numb, while the routine of the quiet house went on outside the library door undisturbed. The chartered yacht still lay at anchor in the lagoon, gazing at its reflection in the still, green water, but the launch remained moored alongside till it shot off in the direction of the open sea in the early afternoon. Another fishing expedition was in progress.

When night fell they could see the lights from the cabin windows shining in the darkness like tiny stars, but the visit of the day before was not repeated.

The following morning Vanessa went down to the beach for a quick swim. She had been typing for over an hour, but Alex had decided to rewrite a paragraph or two before she completed the chapter and she had seized the opportunity to cool off in the deep green water which she found so tempting.

Going through the banana plantation she was in time to see the launch streaking away from the jetty, although she was quite sure that no one from the yacht had been to the house.

Well, they could land for a swim from the beach, she thought, just as she was about to do.

Slipping off her cotton beach-coat, she kicked her sandals aside and plunged into the green lagoon. It was heavenly; warm and yet cool, with hardly a ripple on the surface of the water and the sky so blue overhead that it seemed to stretch for ever. She lay on her back and watched it, floating idly, and then she turned to paddle gently while she gazed down at the gently wavering coral far below. Little coloured fish darted in between the coral stalks, playing hide-and-seek with one another, while big green crabs lumbered past on their sides, their claws waving as if in salute.

When the launch came back across the lagoon she looked up, expecting to see the Schoebergs and, possibly, Diane and Ava Perani, but it was Robin's fair head and scarlet T-shirt which stood out against the gleaming white paintwork of the wheelhouse. He yelled a greeting to her as the launch passed, dousing her with spray.

Shaking the water out of her eyes, she was in time to see Barbie seated in the well with Diane by her side. They were obviously on a joy-ride and Robin was in his element.

One glance at Diane's face had convinced her that the trip on the launch had been well planned beforehand. Barbie took Robin to the beach each morning after breakfast to play there for an hour and nobody asked questions. Barbie was trusted implicitly and Carrie's beach house was near enough for them to go for refreshment if they needed it. It would have been simple enough for Diane to have seen them from the deck of the yacht and to borrow the launch to come ashore. In this way she had made friends with her son.

Well, why not, Vanessa thought, although it would be harder on Robin when his mother sailed away again. Helena had been right about that.

The launch swept past her again before she reached the shore, going more slowly this time, with only Diane aboard. She waved a pink chiffon headscarf in salute, and Vanessa swam on to find Robin and Barbie waiting for her in the shallow water.

'We went on the speedboat!' Robin shouted. 'It can go as fast as a bird. Swoosh! Just like that.' He skimmed the water with his hand. 'I can go again to-morrow, if I like,' he added joyfully.

'Hadn't you better ask your grandmother's permission first?' Vanessa suggested as they made their way up the beach. 'She might wonder where you'd gone, otherwise.'

Robin considered her thoughtfully.

'Yes,' he agreed. 'Barbie will ask.'

Barbie pulled him down on the warm, white sand to put on his shoes.

'Can't walk up through the bananas without them,' she said. 'Yo' get yo' feet all mudded.'

Barbie never kept a thing in her mind for more than five minutes at a time, so Vanessa decided to refresh her memory about the launch.

'Remember to ask Mrs Rossiter about going out in the boat to-morrow,' she prompted as she went to change out of her swim-suit. 'It's best to be sure.'

'I go one quick time right away, Missie Gilbert,' Barbie assured her, her face split in a smile from ear to ear.

Vanessa typed diligently throughout the afternoon. With the jalousies drawn it was cool enough in the library and Alex seemed in a great hurry to get on. Work was a pleasure to her under these circumstances and the time passed quickly, with the sound of activity drifting down from the cane fields to keep her company.

Alex came in at four o'clock, followed by Teresa with a tea tray.

'I thought we would have it in here,' he said. 'You've been working like a Trojan.'

'So have you, apparently.' She indicated the bulky sheaf of MS he had laid on her table. 'You must be nearly finished.'

He plodded to the window and back.

'Almost,' he said. 'I'm not satisfied, of course—one never is—but it reads better after a spell away from it. I'll go over it again once you've finished.'

She judged that it would take her another two weeks to complete her task of re-typing and then it would depend on Alex how long she would remain at La Sola. If he decided that he had to do further revision they would remain on the island until the final draft was complete.

'Why are you smiling?' he asked.

'Was I? I must have been pleased with my thoughts.'

'Do I ask what they were?'

'If you like. I was thinking what a pleasant place La Sola is.'

'You're happy here?'

She hesitated.

'Who wouldn't be happy working under such ideal conditions?'

'That's not what I asked. I wanted to know if you could be happy living in a place like this for the rest of your life. Maybe I'm asking you for a woman's point of view.'

Diane's name flashed across her mind. Was he asking her if Diane should have accepted La Sola in the first place?

'I've always loved solitude,' she admitted, 'but La Sola is isolated, Alex. You found that yourself, I think.'

He sat down at the desk, staring at the confusion of reference books he had left there.

'I couldn't settle,' he said. 'Not after Diane left the island. I wouldn't admit I went after her, but I did. I followed her to New York, sure that I was bound to come across her, but I didn't. I guess she just never made Broadway. Then I heard she was in Europe with some people she had met.'

'And you followed her there, too?'

'Yes and no. I was determined not to be made to look a fool.'

She recognised the streak of Max in him there, the determination passed on to them by Helena, who had never really trusted Diane.

'What are you going to do?' she asked.

'Do?' He stared at her for a moment. 'What can I do? She hasn't changed her ways; she's still sponging off people like the Peranis, who like to be amused.'

Vanessa turned to face him.

'Alex, are *you* going to stay at La Sola?' she asked.

He lit a cheroot, his hands slightly unsteady as he watched her pour the tea.

'I doubt it,' he said. 'I'm not needed here, and after a while Max would make me feel like a parasite, even if I was writing to keep myself and Robin.'

'Have you asked him?'

'No,' he frowned. 'Why should I beg? Max has done all right out of the estate. He's got what he always wanted—freedom to roam the sea. That's all he cares about now, I guess. This lucrative charter business of his is quite something, I gather. Let's hope it's all legal and above board,' he added briskly.

'Surely you're not suggesting—'

'That Max could stoop to anything criminal?' he finished for her. 'Other people have done it, my dear Vanessa, quite frequently and in this day and age. We needn't go back to Henry Morgan for a spot of piracy on the high seas. The Customs around these islands have a whale of a problem, believe me. All sorts of people smuggle all sorts of things, large and small. You only have to think of Cuba to see what I mean.'

'I honestly don't think Max would take such a risk,' she found herself saying, without much justification. 'It would reflect badly on La Sola.'

'You're mighty sure of his motives,' he laughed. 'Has he made love to you?'

A deep colour rushed to her cheeks.

'Why should he?' she managed, remembering that scorching kiss aboard the schooner. 'Max thinks of nothing but work.'

'You could be right,' he agreed, 'but why the confusion? You actually blushed just now!'

'Sometimes you do confuse me, Alex,' she admitted. 'You never seem to be serious for long.'

'I often try to be,' he said, 'but everybody needs

a façade behind which they can hide on occasion. But don't let's worry about it unduly.' He held out his empty plate. ' I'll have another scone.'

She passed him the dish, aware that the conversation had shaken her considerably.

' I'll take you up to the camp to-night,' he promised. ' The cane is almost gathered and there's an air of carnival about.'

She remembered what Max had said about the Limbo dancing and was eager enough to go, although she could not imagine Max joining them to witness the spectacle of carnival which he must have seen many times before.

' Be ready by ten,' Alex advised, ' and take a shawl or something. The camp is fairly high up, so they get the benefit of any wind that's going.'

There was little wind, however, by the time they set out. The lagoon was a deep, cobalt blue under a new moon and the slanting palms laid dark shadows on the yellow sand. Deeper shadows stretched upwards from the banana grove to the edge of the garden and the shadow of the house itself was darkest of all.

They climbed upwards into the valley, passing the slain sugar cane before they came, at last, to the trees. Ahead of them they could see the camp site, with dark figures silhouetted against the orange glow from the fires.

A long avenue of regularly-spaced poles carried kerosene flares to light the path, converging eventually on a clearing where the workers were already gathering. They were mostly young, with here and there a sprinkling of older men who had come to watch and clap their hands to the rhythm of calypso. All were gaily attired, the young men in tight, colourful trousers which seemed to be stuck on to their limbs, the girls in wide-skirted dresses with bright bandanas binding their heads and large gold rings dangling from their ears. In one corner a steel band was tuning up, a primitive affair of oil drums and guitars which produced a great deal of noise but were greatly appreciated by those present. Everybody chattered and laughed above the din.

'It's a bit like a monkey-house in a zoo,' Alex remarked, 'but they'll settle down to the real business of Limbo after a while. Where would you like to sit?'

'Won't they resent us?' Vanessa asked. 'After all, it's a private sort of celebration, isn't it?'

'Everybody's welcome,' Alex assured her. 'They won't mind a bit. On the contrary, they'll be flattered and ask you to join in the dancing.'

They sat on the edge of the clearing, eyed shyly by the dark-skinned throng, but apparently nothing could dampen the native ardour. The dancing began almost immediately, slowly at first, with only a few couples stamping out the rhythm on the baked earth of the clearing, but presently they were joined by others until almost everyone was taking part.

They danced barefooted, waving their arms to the pattern of Limbo, the light from the flares reflected in their eyes, the bare torsos of the men gleaming as they moved in and out between the trees. Two poles were produced with a cross-bar to lay between them and the dancers stood aside to make way for the experts.

Vanessa held her breath as a tall youth sprang into the clearing, followed by another and then by a girl with her hair tightly bound about her head. An oil-soaked rag was tied to the centre of the cross-bar and lit from a nearby flare as the two youths swung into the dance. They turned and gyrated in a wild ecstasy as the steel band beat out the music and presently the girl joined in, her skirts held high, her dark eyes flashing as she circled each in turn. Vanessa looked away for a moment. In this primitive form of the dance she was reminded of Alex and Max with a younger Diane taunting each in turn.

Suddenly she felt Alex stiffen at her side.

'We've got the yacht party,' he said beneath his breath.

The gleam of a white dress was visible between the trees and Diane came forward to the edge of the clearing, followed by Ava Perani and her husband. The

153

Schoebergs were a few paces behind. We're all here, Vanessa thought, except Max.

She saw him then, standing well back beyond the dancers, half-hidden in the shadow of the trees, and her pulses raced as the drums began to roll.

The scene was almost primitive as the dancers came, one by one, towards the flaming cross-bar and the tension spread out over the clearing to engulf them all. The black bodies twisted and swayed, bending backwards to shuffle under the bar. Again and again they returned to glide beneath it as it was lowered gradually nearer and nearer to the ground.

Vanessa glanced across at Max, but he made no sign that he had seen them. Diane and the Peranis had come up behind them.

'Exciting,' Ava Perani murmured. 'How do they do it without burning themselves?'

'Sometimes they do,' Alex said abruptly.

The girl gave up first . She had wormed her way under the bar until the flames appeared to sear her face and now she left the final achievement to the men. Both youths cleared the bar at only inches from the ground, still moving their feet to the rhythm of the dance.

Wild applause greeted their achievement as the tension eased, but Vanessa found herself unable to clap with the others. Max came across the clearing to where they sat.

'It's fantastic!' Laureen Schoeberg exclaimed. 'But there's something about it worries me—a sort of primitive bravado that could so easily turn to tragedy.'

'All challenge is primitive,' Max said, 'and these people are expressing it in the medium they know best. This is just a practice run, by the way. The more startling exhibitions will be reserved for the final carnival, when all the sugar is safely in. They dress up then in fantastic costumes, with beaded and feathered headdresses and gruesome masks to complete the illusion of devils, which are always conquered in the dance. It's quite a spectacle, but you won't see it till the moon is full.'

'We won't be staying that long,' Carlo Perani said regretfully. 'I have a cable from Philadelphia, calling me back there. Business, you know,' he added, as if it was something he had just remembered.

Alex looked swiftly in Diane's direction, but she was already on her feet, preparing to dance with Henry Schoeberg.

The entertainment would go on far into the night, but the spirit of carnival had gone. They all seemed to feel it, and Vanessa was glad when Alex suggested that they should go down.

'To-morrow we have work to do,' he said.

He had danced once with Diane, holding her loosely in his arms, the brief contact obviously upsetting him.

'Diane should have stayed away,' he muttered as they went back down the path.

Max walked behind them, guiding Mrs Perani over the rough places.

'We had to come up,' she explained. 'We saw the lights from the yacht and Diane said the dancing would be worth while. It was a wonderful experience, wasn't it? But there,' she remembered, 'you've seen it all before!'

'Many times,' Max assured her.

'And taken part in it?'

'Once,' he admitted darkly.

'Does it happen all the time?' she wanted to know.

'When the sugar is in, yes.'

'It's just fantastic,' she repeated. 'The rhythm never stops, even when their bodies are only an inch or two from the flame. I'm glad I saw it in the raw, so to speak, and not all fixed up as a tourist attraction in some hotel garden.'

'Even there,' Max told her, 'it has its own particular type of challenge.'

'I'm sure,' she agreed, holding tightly on to his arm.

They stopped in front of the house, expecting to be invited in for a nightcap. Max left Alex to make the decision.

'You'll have a drink before you go?' Alex asked.

'Mrs Perani doesn't look too warm.'

'I always wilt a bit after midnight, and especially if there's been a lot of excitement,' Ava declared, 'but we'd be pleased to have that drink, I guess. Your mother won't be disturbed?' she asked as they made their way along the verandah.

'She'll have been asleep for the best part of four hours,' Alex said. 'She knew where we were going and she wouldn't expect us back much before this.'

They sprawled in the verandah chairs, tired after their walk from the valley, while Vanessa went with Alex to bring the drinks.

'Do you think we should make coffee?' he asked. 'It would take longer.'

'I could make it while you poured the drinks,' Vanessa suggested. 'Mrs Perani did look cold.'

'She's got no flesh on her,' Alex growled. 'All American woman are the same.'

'You know you don't mean that,' she smiled. 'You're just—put out about something.'

'Am I?' He turned to look at her. 'Maybe you're right.'

It was becoming a habit with her to make coffee in the deserted kitchens after the servants had gone, Vanessa thought, setting out cups and saucers on a tray, but she was surprised when Max came to carry her burden on to the verandah for her. He stood looking at her for several minutes before he spoke.

'Did you enjoy yourself?' he asked.

'Very much. It has been a night to remember,' she answered.

Walking ahead of him through the silent hall, she trod lightly not to disturb Helena, but suddenly Max's mother was standing in the doorway of her bedroom looking at them. She wore a long blue housecoat and her hair was loosely knotted behind her head, as if she had just put it up.

'I heard you come in,' she said. 'I wasn't asleep. Carrie and I went to bed early and I've had my four hours.' She smiled at her son. 'I take it the sugar is almost in?'

156

'Not far to go now,' he assured her, offering her an answering smile. 'Do you feel like joining us?'

She glanced at the tray.

'We've got company, I see.'

'Diane and the people from the yacht.'

Helena straightened her shoulders.

'I'll come out,' she said.

Their visitors stayed for an hour.

'We may not see you again,' Ava Perani said, holding out her hand when they were ready to go, 'so let me say a big "thank you" for your hospitality, Mrs Rossiter. It was sure kind of you to have us in your home.'

Helena murmured something about it being a pleasure, waiting for them to say their final goodbyes and leave, and Alex took down a hurricane lamp to guide them to the beach. Max disappeared into the shadows around the house as Vanessa began to gather up the coffee cups.

'Leave these till the morning,' Helena commanded. 'The girls will clear them away.'

She took Vanessa's arm, leaning heavily on it as they entered the quiet house, and La Sola seemed to hold out its arms to both of them.

'How still it is now,' Vanessa murmured. 'Even the crickets have stopped chirping.'

'They feel the dawn.' Helena paused to look about her as if she were seeing La Sola for the first time. 'This old house is too big for me,' she sighed. 'When Max marries I plan to go to the beach house with Carrie. We could be there together. I'm not going to get any stronger, but I don't think I'm going to die yet awhile.'

'I'm sure you're not,' Vanessa told her.

'I'd like to see Max happily married.' Helena paused by the library door. 'Is that too much to ask?'

'No.'

The bleak little monosyllable was as much as Vanessa could manage and when Helena had closed her door between them she hurried to her room before Alex could return.

The yacht pulled out of the lagoon the following morning. Vanessa saw it go from the library window where she had been typing for more than an hour. She had also watched Robin go down to the beach with Barbie, but half an hour later she thought she heard them returning through the garden.

Everyone had been late getting up after their midnight trip to the valley and Alex had decided to work in his room. He had come into the library in dressing-gown and slippers, complaining about the heat, but she imagined that there might be another reason for his restlessness.

'I'm going to do something about that last chapter, after all,' he announced. 'What, I don't know at the present moment, but you needn't type it, since it would be a waste of time. I might just scrap it altogether.'

'I thought it was rather good,' she ventured.

'It was ordinary.' He frowned. 'Nothing's going right, is it?' he demanded. 'Even my work—'

'Could I do anything to help?' she asked.

He regarded her vaguely.

'You? No, not really; you're helping as it is.'

There seemed nothing more to be said; if there was anything she could do, Alex would ask.

'Go for a swim,' he advised. 'You look flushed.'

'I'd rather finish the typescript,' she decided.

He paused beside her chair.

'What are you going to do when you go back to England?' he asked. 'When all this is over?'

'I'll find another job, I expect.' She almost choked over the words.

'Would you like to take me on as a full-time boss?'

'If you needed me, but you said yesterday that you wouldn't start another novel right away,' she reminded him.

'I need to work.' His voice was suddenly harsh. 'But that's for the future. Go and have your swim, Vanessa, and we'll talk about it some other time.'

She decided to take his advice, feeling the pain in her neck muscles again after two hours' steady typing. I sit badly, she decided, all tensed up and worrying about getting things done.

It was easy to relax in the water, although she felt the emptiness of the lagoon in a new way now. It seemed to stretch out endlessly, like her own future, with nothing on the horizon as far as she could see. Out towards the reef there was a single line of white foam where the waves broke against the coral, but that was all. Max, she thought. Max! Am I never to feel your arms about me again? Must I go on living in an emptiness like this without you?

When she turned her head she was drifting towards the shallows at the foot of the Bluff, yet she could hear the waves pounding ahead of her among the rocks where the current could pull her away. Max had warned her about the Bluff.

Swimming strongly, she was back in the safety of the lagoon again where the yacht had anchored for three brief days.

Was that all? It seemed like a lifetime, and perhaps their lives had been changed by its coming.

Drying herself in the sun, she remembered Diane, wondering about her and unable to understand why she had come back to La Sola to go off again so quickly.

It was a great temptation to linger on the beach, but she knew that the lunch bell would go at one o'clock. They pleased themselves where they ate their midday meal and she decided to have hers on her verandah. Barbie would bring it on a tray, salad and some fruit freshly picked off the trees. It was enough in this sudden, humid heat, she decided, mopping her brow as she came out of the comparative shade of the banana grove and moved towards the house.

It was then, for the first time, that she became aware of the general confusion. The girls were running about, chattering fearfully, while the sound of violent sobbing came from the kitchen premises.

'What is it?' she asked. 'What has happened?'

Teresa gazed at her with mournful eyes.

'It's Barbie,' she said. 'She done gone lost young Master Robin.'

'Lost him?' Vanessa's mind rushed ahead to the possible meaning of the girl's words. 'Where have they gone?'

Barbie, she done gone nowhere.' Teresa gazed in awe towards the kitchen. 'She jus' howl her head off an' say she never seed him no more when they came from the beach.'

This was serious, and Vanessa's first thought was for Helena.

'Mrs Rossiter,' she said. 'Where is she, Teresa?'

'She go rest awhile,' the girl answered.

No one could be 'resting' with that din going on, Vanessa decided.

'Tell Barbie to be quiet and come to the sitting-room,' she ordered. 'We must *do* something. Have you seen Mr Alex?'

Teresa looked alarmed.

'He goin' skin Barbie alive, Miss Gilbert,' she announced solemnly. 'That's why she howl so loud.'

Vanessa hurried towards the library to find the door wide open and the desk in disarray. Alex was nowhere to be seen.

When Barbie finally crossed the hall to the sitting-room Vanessa followed her in.

'Barbie, try to stop this awful noise,' she pleaded. 'It won't help and nobody is going to punish you for something that may have been an accident.'

Two large black eyes brimming with tears regarded her suspiciously for a moment.

'You goin' blame me, too?' Barbie asked.

'Nobody is going to blame you if you couldn't help what happened,' Vanessa tried to reason, 'but I can't give you any sort of answer till I know what you have done. How could you have "lost" Master Robin between here and the beach?'

'Ah jus' don' know, Miss Gilbert, ma'am. Ah jus' plain baffled.' The tears rolled down the fat black cheeks. 'One minute that chil' there, the next he no' there. Ah jus' done turn ma head for one minute an' he disappear.'

'Where?' Vanessa demanded, taking a really serious

160

view of the situation now. ' Were you near the house?'

Barbie looked down at her toes.

' We was in the bananas,' she said.

Barbie was almost fifteen, a well-developed, comely young girl who already attracted the admiring glances of the plantation workers, and it wasn't hard to guess what had happened. On the way up from the beach Barbie had lingered for a moment with her latest beau and Robin had gone ahead through the bananas towards La Sola or back towards the beach.

A sudden vision of the deserted beach and empty lagoon quickened her pulses and sent the colour into her cheeks.

' Was there anyone on the beach while you were there?' she demanded. ' Any stranger—or perhaps someone you knew?'

Barbie shook her head.

' Ah see no one,' she sobbed. ' Maybe some bad spirit done take Master Robin away.'

' Don't talk nonsense!' Vanessa knew that she would get no further with the frightened girl and probably Alex had already asked all these questions. Barbie was almost in a state of shock and no doubt he had threatened her because he was also taking Robin's disappearance seriously.

For the next half-hour Vanessa searched the gardens without result, checking up on Rosalind, who was peacefully grazing behind the house, and combing all the nooks and crannies where a small boy might be hiding, but finally she had to return to the house to admit defeat. Alex came along the verandah to meet her like a tornado let loose.

' Where have you been?' he demanded.

' Searching for Robin, and before that I was on the beach.'

He looked afraid.

' Of course you know what's happened,' he said. ' Diane's taken him.'

' Alex, you have to be absolutely sure!'

He caught her arm.

' I know what I'm talking about,' he declared. ' I

know Diane. We've searched this place from end to end. There isn't even a hollow in a tree we haven't looked into. We've been searching for over an hour, ever since Barbie came back, but she had missed Robin before that and *hid*, of all things! Too afraid— too ashamed, if you like, to admit she'd been eyeing the boys instead of doing her job.'

'You frightened her,' Vanessa said quietly, 'by threatening to skin her alive. I might be able to get something out of her now that she's quietened down a little.'

'What's the use?' he wanted to know. 'You don't have to think very far before you come to Diane. I should have known she would do this. The yacht went out this morning and Robin went with it.'

'Do you think he would go without a murmur?'

'Willingly or unwillingly, he's on that yacht!'

Vanessa held her breath. He seemed so certain, so utterly convinced that it was impossible to argue with him.

'What are you going to do?' she asked.

His jaw tightened, making him look like Max.

'Go after her.' He glanced quickly at his watch. 'There's a freighter going out at three o'clock. With a bit of luck I can board her.' He hesitated. 'Tell my mother what you have to and break it gently to her—but make her understand that I am bringing Robin back here. She worries about him.'

'Couldn't you take the schooner?' she asked.

He shook his head.

'The crew will be ashore, scattered around the island or working with Max on the cane. The freighter is the best idea.'

He had made up his mind, even to the final detail, she realised, unable to detain him any longer, although a small, persistent doubt nagged at the back of her mind. She had been on the beach and she hadn't noticed anything untoward. If Diane had spirited Robin away it must have been much earlier than Barbie had admitted.

'When did they go to the beach?' she asked.

'About nine o'clock, Barbie said, and they came away at twelve.'

By twelve o'clock Vanessa had been on her way to the lagoon and the yacht had gone, which meant that Alex could be going on the freighter on a wild goose chase. She could not presume to deter him, however; he was an angry, worried man.

'Have you seen Max?' she asked. 'There's just a chance Robin could be with him.'

He shook his head.

'Max went back to Grenada with the sugar buyers,' he explained. 'Nobody's here when they're needed.' He clenched his fists. 'I'll do this in my own way, Vanessa, but you can help by explaining everything to my mother, if you will?'

He was more rational now, speaking calmly for the first time.

'I can't say how sorry I am,' she told him, 'but do take care, Alex. Don't do anything rash.'

He turned away.

'I won't, but I mean to get Robin back. This is his home.'

She watched him go, a tall, determined figure striding out into the humidity of the sultry afternoon without a hat and with only a small briefcase in his hand. He had stuffed pyjamas and a toothbrush into it as they talked and now he was ready to follow Diane to the ends of the earth, if need be. He had even taken his passport from the drawer in the desk and all the money he kept there.

Why would Diane do such a thing? Why? Why? But there was no reasoning to explain a mother's actions when she felt that she needed her child and was being deliberately deprived of him. Vindictiveness had nothing to do with it.

Half dreading her meeting with Helena, Vanessa walked slowly towards the bedroom to find Carrie Hazeltine already there.

'I've just told her,' Carrie whispered, coming across the big, airy room to meet her in the doorway. 'She's shocked, but not unduly so.'

'We must organise a thorough search,' Helena decided from the far side of the room. 'Little boys have been "lost" before at La Sola and been no further than the village or the caves.'

'The caves?' Vanessa repeated. 'Where are they?'

'They're half-way up the mountain,' Carrie explained.

The mountain, Vanessa thought. What was it about the mountain that kept troubling her mind?

'Has Max come in?' Helena asked.

'He left for Grenada early,' Carrie told her. 'The agent came about the sugar and Max went back to St George with him. They'll be here again in the morning.'

It was foolish to think of Robin being with Max under the circumstances, Vanessa decided, but the thought persisted as they continued their search. The heat had become more and more oppressive as the day lengthened and a coppery tinge lay across the sky. The blue faded out of the lagoon and a wind disturbed the palms, a hot wind breathing fire into their faces as they turned them towards the mountain.

Vanessa was never quite sure afterwards when she decided that she must go up there. Ever since they had spoken about Max she had been aware of the connection between him and the mountain in her own mind. He had promised to take Robin up there one day.

'I have to go,' she told Carrie, 'but don't upset Mrs Rossiter by telling her.'

'You can't go alone,' Carrie declared emphatically. 'I wouldn't allow it. The mountain is no place for a woman to go climbing without help.'

'I'll take Napoleon,' Vanessa assured her.

'See that you do.' Carrie was still not very sure about the need to go on searching the island. 'I'm coming round to the idea that Alex was right,' she confessed. 'Diane has got him.'

'Perhaps,' Vanessa allowed, 'but we have to go on searching.'

'Don't forget to take Napoleon,' Carrie warned.

'We don't want you lost on the mountain into the bargain. And there's just one thing,' she added. 'Don't go any higher than the caves.'

Vanessa collected Napoleon after she had put a few biscuits and some chocolate into a paper bag in case they did find Robin, who was sure to be hungry. The old Negro had climbed the mountain many times, but he shook his head when she suggested that Robin might have gone as far as the caves.

'He would get tired and lie down long before he got there,' he said in his carefully thought out English. 'The caves is a long way up.'

At first they climbed in bright sunshine, but presently the trees thickened and they were in their shade. Napoleon forged on ahead, following a defined path and calling back to her every now and then to make sure that she was following him. It was difficult going for Vanessa, who was unused to so much exercise in the heat, and very soon she was bathed in perspiration. It trickled like a small rivulet between her shoulder-blades and stood in drops along the line of her upper lip while her hair clung damply to her forehead and the palms of her hands became moist. It was ridiculous to assume that a small boy of five could have climbed so far, she decided.

Napoleon pressed on, his black face turned towards the crater.

'I think we ought to go back,' she suggested. 'It's all been—a great mistake.'

He retraced his steps down the path to where she stood.

'Soon we reach the caves,' he promised. 'Big storm him coming up over sea.'

He pointed downwards through a gap in the trees where they could see the lagoon. It was the colour of slate, with no clearly defined line between the water and the sky, and all the surface was broken by angry little waves hurrying towards the Bluff where they dashed themselves to pieces against the rocks.

The first spots of rain fell even as they looked, pattering down on the trees and soaking through to them. It was warm, heavy rain, splashing with a loud sound on the branches above their heads, penetrating the thick canopy of the leaves in next to no time.

'We must shelter,' Vanessa said.

'The caves,' Napoleon suggested. 'We could go to the caves.'

They crossed a mountain stream that would soon be swollen by the rain, coming out of the comparative shelter of the trees on to a rocky scree which stretched for the remainder of the way right up to the crater. Napoleon climbed slowly and steadily, saving his breath, but presently he turned along the slope towards a group of rocks in the rough scrub. The rain, which had come across the lagoon with the trade wind, lashed against them with vicious intent, screaming and howling among the scrub as the sun went in behind the thick bank of cloud which had formed on the mountain top while they climbed through the trees. It was so cold now that Vanessa could not suppress a shiver.

'We go quick,' Napoleon urged. 'Some dam' bad storm on its way perhaps.'

Telling herself how foolish she had been to come so far on a false trail, Vanessa scrambled after him, already half exhausted by the rigours of their climb. From oppressive heat to chill rain, they had run the gamut of the elements to find themselves high on the mountain above La Sola yet out of sight or sound of it. Ahead of them she could see the caves, but they looked as uninviting as the chill world outside. Another sudden shower of rain thudded on the ground all round them, sending them running for shelter.

'Quickly, Napoleon!' she cried. 'Don't get too wet.'

They were already drenched and chilled to the marrow by the vicious raindrops which had pattered down through the trees. This was a different world, far removed from the comforts of La Sola and the pink coral beaches which skirted the lagoons. Up here anything could happen, Vanessa thought. The mountain seemed the personification of cruelty, with its dark face turned to the leaden sky.

166

'Look here!' Napoleon cried, already in the cave and bending over a small figure curled up at the foot of a rock. 'Hey, Miss Gilbert, ma'am, we've found him after all! We've found the little master!'

Sudden unreasonable fear gripped Vanessa by the throat.

'Is he—all right?'

'He's asleep. He must have climbed all this way by himself.' The old Negro's voice was full of admiration. 'I know for sure he was a fine little fellow long ago! He going to be like Mister Max one of these days, yo' just mark my words!'

Robin had stirred and Vanessa was on her knees beside him.

'My head hurts,' he complained sleepily, not quite fully aware of where he was.

'You must have fallen.' She took him into her arms, smoothing the tangled hair back from his eyes to reveal a cut on the side of his brow. His knees were also grazed and the white shirt he wore was stained with mud. 'What happened?'

'I slipped. All the stones rolled away and I fell. A big tree stopped me.'

'Oh, Robbie!' She held him closer. 'I'm glad we found you.'

It was all she could think of to say, and anything else she might have added would have been carried away in the first peal of thunder as the storm finally struck the mountain.

Never had she seen such rain, never before had she felt the ground tremble beneath her as it did now, as if the whole mountain was ready to erupt at any moment. The rain gathered on the rocks at the mouth of the caves and poured down the slope towards the trees in a raging torrent, carrying stones and scrub along with it, and the thunder-claps seemed to be right above their heads.

They were safe in the caves, however, and they were also comparatively dry. Napoleon lit a fire with some of the scrub and they warmed their hands at it and ate the biscuits and chocolate Vanessa had brought with her. Robin ate ravenously, still holding on to her hand.

'You won't leave me, will you?' he asked. 'You won't go away like my mother did.'

Vanessa's heart contracted with pity.

'Your mother will come back,' she soothed him. Honestly, Robbie, she'll come back one day.'

She realised that she believed what she had just said, although she had no justification for the comforting statement. Diane would return—for Alex or Max.

'Can we go home now?' Robin wanted to know.

'Not just yet.' Vanessa looked out through the mouth of the cave to where the rain was still pouring down as if it would never stop. 'We would get dreadfully wet, and we'll make quicker time when it clears.'

Napoleon turned in her direction, his black eyes full of concern.

'This dam' rain never stop!' he declared in the idiom of his race. 'We goin' be up here for one very long time, Miss Gilbert, ma'am. I go down the mountain soon, when that black devil thunder stop hammering up there.'

He cast his eyes towards the angry heavens and Vanessa saw his mouth fall open.

'What is it, Napoleon?' she asked, trying to keep her voice from rising.

He pointed up towards the crater, which she could not see from the interior of the cave.

'Big mist,' he said laconically.

Vanessa went to stand beside him, peering through the slackening rain. Almost directly above them the clouds were rolling down the mountainside, obliterating the summit in a grey, impenetrable blanket which moved steadily towards them. She remained looking at it in horror.

'It could take hours to lift,' she murmured.

Napoleon looked round at Robin who was tossing the few remaining sticks on the fire.

'I go right away,' he decided.

'No.' Vanessa held him back. 'I won't let you take

such a risk, Napoleon. We'll have to sit it out here and hope this will roll away as quickly as it came.'

He nodded, quite frankly afraid of the thunder because the superstitions of his ancestors remained strong in his blood. Vanessa knew that the mist clouds were the greater hazard, but they would be safe while they remained in the caves.

She tried to entertain Robin by playing a game with him, thankful that he was not afraid of the thunder, but soon it was five o'clock and he was hungry again. The biscuits and chocolate had sustained him for a little while, but now he was greatly in need of a hot meal to make him feel secure. She took off her light jacket to wrap it round his shoulders.

'I look funny!' he laughed, waving his skinny arms in the long sleeves. 'It's too big for me.' He attempted to take it off.

'I'd keep it on, if I were you,' Vanessa advised. 'It's going to be quite cold before long.'

The red lower lip pouted.

'I want to go home,' Robin announced once more.

She put her arms about him, cradling him against the warmth of her own body.

'So you shall,' she told him, 'but we may have to sleep here. We could go down at any minute, though, if the clouds go away.'

The rain had slackened and Napoleon had managed to find some more scrub to burn. It was wet, but it caught after a while, making a welcome light in the cave.

From time to time they peered through the drifting cloud blanket, hoping that it was about to lift, but it continued to swirl past the mouth of the cave, obliterating even the nearest shrub in time. The trees below them were completely hidden and there was no sign of the path.

The sudden tropic dark descended on them within minutes and they were doubly glad of the light from the fire. They played a game, throwing sticks on to it as they counted.

An hour later Vanessa looked up to find that

Napoleon had gone. He had slipped out into that deadly mist to seek assistance for them, but the chances were that he would never reach La Sola alive. Napoleon Bonaparte Wilkinson had been named from a packet of razor blades which his mother had found on a rubbish heap, but he had the courage of a lion.

Tears dimmed Vanessa's eyes as she thought of him, of the hazardous journey he had undertaken to save his master's child, and she could only pray that the demons of the mountain would not notice him. He had no aid to guide him down the slippery path towards the trees, only his native instinct which would have to feel the way, inch by treacherous inch.

Towards eight o'clock Robin fell asleep. Completely worn out, he accepted the comfort of Vanessa's arms and the warmth of her woollen jacket. Sitting without movement, she felt the cold seeping into her body as the fire died out for want of fuel. The wood ash still glowed, but soon that, too, would die. An eerie stillness had gathered in the cave which seemed to press in on her with the slow passing of time, a sort of grim waiting which had nothing to do with hope. When she finally moved her position a little she almost cried out with pain. A paralysing cramp seized her limbs, but she could not move the sleeping child in her arms in case Robin should become afraid. It was just possible that he would sleep quite peacefully throughout the night.

She dozed and woke again, and the silence was still all around her. It seemed, too, that the mist had come right into the cave, penetrating like a grey, searching wraith now that the fire had gone out. She bit her lip. This was worse than she had imagined. Robin chuckled in his sleep and she moved him to ease the pain in her arms, wondering again about Napoleon, who was no longer a young man, out there in the grey blanket of cloud. If he had managed to keep to the path all might be well with him, but if he had strayed from it or fallen in the darkness he might be lying out there somewhere on the mountain injured and unable to move.

Towards midnight she thought that she heard the sound of running feet, but it was an illusion. Like all the other chimeras of the tropic night, the sound had been conjured up out of her imagination to taunt the failing courage which seemed to be deserting her and making her wonder if they would ever be rescued alive.

Thrusting the daunting thought aside, she tried to visualise the mountain bathed in sunlight with its wealth of lush vegetation spilling down to the valley floor. If there were clouds they would be sailing high to leave the great conical peak of the extinct volcano silhouetted against the blue of the Caribbean sky. A light trade wind would ruffle the palms and fill the sails of the little yachts, and Max would be taking the schooner out to cross to Grenada or Martinique or wherever he wished to go.

Foolish thoughts, perhaps, but immensely comforting in her present perilous state.

The first indication that help might be at hand was no more than a trickle of falling stones. She heard them rumbling down the scree in front of the caves and knew that someone was approaching their shelter. The heavy footsteps came rapidly along the path and Max was standing in the pale aperture of the cave. For a moment she could not believe that he was really there.

' Max—!'

He blocked out all the light as he stooped to enter.

'Are you all right?' he asked harshly.

' Yes—yes, we're safe,' she whispered, hardly believing that he could have come so swiftly. ' Robin has been asleep for a long time.'

He set down the hurricane lamp he carried and lifted the child from her knees.

' Napoleon got to La Sola an hour ago,' he said, his voice not very clear. ' He was totally exhausted, but he was able to tell me where you were.' He laid Robin down, still asleep, on the coat he had brought and turned towards her, his expression harsh in the yellow light from the lamp. ' It was a damned silly thing to do,' he informed her.

'It was the only thing I could do.' She tried to rise, but her cramped limbs would not support her. 'I had a feeling Robin had come up here.'

She was kneeling on the earthen floor of the cave, unable to raise herself further, and he bent swiftly, taking her by the shoulders to support her. She leaned heavily against him, suddenly shaking from head to foot.

'All right,' he said quite gently, 'you won through, but you might not have done. You know nothing about this mountain.'

A flood of tears seemed to be dammed up in her heart, but she was unable to shed them. Max had no use for the sort of woman who went to pieces in an emergency. She pushed him away from her, leaning against the cold rock face.

'We must see to Robin,' she told him unsteadily.

Max pulled out a flask, pouring a measure of thick black liquid into the silver stopper-cap.

'The only remedy,' he said, holding it out to her. 'Drink it down. It'll do you a power of good.'

The rum was hot and dark and bitter, but she managed to swallow it obediently, although it brought tears to her eyes.

'What about Napoleon?' she asked.

'He'll be all right, but he's too old a man to go climbing on a mountain or wandering off it in a mist. His loving family will keep him in bed for a day or two, I expect, and he'll live to tell the tale of your adventure till he's a hundred!'

'Don't joke about it, Max,' she begged. 'He could have died. I didn't want him to leave the cave, but he just disappeared while—while I was playing a little game with Robin. He's a magnificent old man in every sense of the word and I'll never be able to repay him.'

'Just say thank you in your pretty way.' He stood with the flask poised, waiting for her to finish her drink. 'That will be compensation enough for Napoleon, I'm sure.'

172

'Alex went in search of Diane,' she rushed on. 'He thought she had taken Robin off in the yacht with the Peranis, but I had a feeling he might have come up here. He told me he wanted to climb the mountain; he said you had promised to take him "one day", but perhaps he was trying to show you how good he was—that he could climb by himself. Boys do that sort of thing to impress the people they admire.'

His eyes searched her face, as if he were looking for some truth which still evaded him, and then he laughed.

'The rum has made you talkative already,' he said. 'It should also have warmed you through by now.'

'I feel a great deal better,' she admitted.

He sat down on the floor, hugging his knees with the flask still in his hands.

'We'll have to wait,' he announced. 'The cloud is lifting, but it will be dawn before we can see the path properly. You may be able to get some sleep.'

She shook her head.

'I know I won't.'

He poured another measure of rum.

'Try this,' he suggested, but she shook her head.

'One was enough!'

The rum was beginning to have its effects, however. In a moment or two her eyelids closed and the feeling of surrender was absolute. Sleep was the answer to a good many things, she decided drowsily.

She fancied that Max pulled her towards him and she slept with her head on his shoulder, but when the strong dawn light penetrating the cave woke her he was standing looking down at Robin, who was stirring into wakefulness.

'He's going to remember this as a great adventure for a very long time,' he said.

He did not look at her as he gathered their belongings together and blew out the hurricane-lamp, and Vanessa took Robin by the hand and stepped into the morning sun.

CHAPTER VIII

The clouds had all gone from the mountain by the time they reached the tree line and the early morning air was fresh and clear. They could see the whole lagoon stretching before them, with green and turquoise shadows lying on its surface like a watermark on silk. The wind that had blown the clouds away swayed the branches above their heads, helping the sun to dry the leaves, and far out beyond the Bluff they could make out the graceful lines of the schooner lying in the bay among a small flotilla of yachts.

'You came back very quickly,' Vanessa said, remembering Carrie's remark about Max's possible return from Grenada. 'Your aunt didn't expect you till this morning.'

'There was no need for me to stay in St George's.' Max's brow creased in a frown. 'I came back as quickly as I could and we had a following wind all the way, blowing us home.'

It was the same trade wind that had brought the storm clouds to the mountain, Vanessa thought.

'Is that where the saying comes from?' she asked. '"It's an ill wind that blows nobody any good"?'

'I wouldn't be at all surprised!'

They were half-way to La Sola and Robin was already tired. Max lifted him on to his shoulders and they marched on with the child's fingers clutching his thick shock of black hair. It curled at the ends where the wind had ruffled it and this new image of him made him look years younger, endearing him to her in a new and heartbreaking way. He loved this child and he would love his own.

When they finally reached La Sola the entire household was there to greet them. Helena stood at the edge of the verandah, shading her eyes against the sun, with Carrie beside her and the entire kitchen staff ranged in a chattering throng along the garden path. Barbie was there, too, about to weep all over again as soon as she was spoken to, but Robin held out his arms to her and instantly her face was wreathed in smiles.

'Look after him a little better,' Max said as he surrendered his charge.

Helena had decided not to make a fuss of her grandson, although she had spent an anxious night worrying about him.

'The least said, soonest mended,' she declared. 'It was really all Barbie's fault, although we could impress on Robbie that the mountain is no place to go alone. "Even Vanessa took Napoleon with her" ought to do the trick!'

'How is Napoleon?' Vanessa asked.

'Sleeping. I must try to repay him,' Helena declared. 'A good servant is worth his weight in gold these days. Now I suppose it's up to us to make sure that no one gets a chill,' she added practically. 'I'll order hot drinks all round.'

'I'm already full of rum!' Vanessa smiled. 'Max insisted.'

Helena looked round at her son.

'We must try to get in touch with Alex,' she suggested. 'Heaven knows how far he might go in search of the Peranis' yacht.'

Max promised to see to it.

'I can contact Barbados. It's more than likely that the Peranis will have called in there on their way north.'

'Mr Peranis said he had been recalled,' Carrie remembered. 'He'll be on his way back to Philadelphia by now, I should imagine.'

'Probably the others would stay aboard,' Max reflected. 'In any case, I'll try Bridgetown. They ought to know if the yacht is still in the Careenage.'

He went off to make his enquiries and Vanessa made her way to her own room. Her adventure on the mounain had exhausted her, but she could not take advantage of Helena's suggestion to lie down for a while. Thoughts were chasing each other round and round in her head, thoughts of Alex and Diane, but

mostly thoughts of Max. There was the sure knowledge, too, that she would soon have to leave La Sola
if Alex didn't come back. When Max eventually con-
tacted him to say that Robin was safe he might even
send for her to take his books and the almost completed MS back to London. It would all be over then,
her little adventure in the sun and her love for Max.
She might never see him again, but seeing him and
loving him and knowing herself unloved was no better
a fate surely. She would have to leave La Sola some
time; sooner or later Max would watch her sail away,
with mixed feelings, perhaps, because they had come
to know each other a little better, but certainly not
with love.

How could she expect love when she had come here
with Alex to find him mourning Diane?

The house settled back into its habitual peace until
the lunch bell rang. After a refreshing sleep Robin
was quite recovered from his adventure and during
the meal he was bright and questioning.

'Where has everyone gone?' he wanted to know.
'Uncle Max and my father and mother?'

Max still came first, Vanessa noticed.

'They'll be back soon,' Helena assured him without
a great deal of conviction. 'Off you go and feed
Rosalind and then you can take her for a little ride
along the hard.' She held up a cautioning finger.
'But remember, you must take someone with you. No
going off on your own again up the mountain, or
anywhere else!'

Her grandson regarded her thoughtfully.

'No,' he agreed after a moment, 'no going off without someone!'

Barbie was in temporary disgrace. She had served
the meal with a sober countenance, her habitual ear-
to-ear grin sadly missing, and now she was helping to
clear the table, well aware that she would be consigned
to kitchen duties for a week, at least. It would mean
no more romping on the sands as far as she was
concerned, no more searching for fallen coconuts to
pierce and drink their milk in the sun, no more splash-

ing thigh-deep in the cool green water of the lagoon while Robin shrieked with laughter, no more boy-friends hidden behind the banana fronds. In short, no more fun, unless she was permitted to go to the valley dancing by the end of the week of carnival.

Barbie sighed, aware that she deserved some sort of punishment for neglecting her duty, and her heart turned cold when she imagined what might have happened up there on the mountain. Robin could have died, she thought, or been spirited away, and Barbie would have been to blame. Oh, dear lord, what a wicked child Barbie is, to be sure!

She went out with her tray and Helena turned towards the verandah.

'You ought to get some rest,' Carrie told her.

'Rest?' Helena turned to look at her sister-in-law. 'I don't want to lie in bed, just thinking. All this may make a great difference to our life at La Sola, Carrie, and I've got to know—immediately.' Suddenly her whole body tensed as she halted at the top of the steps. 'The yacht is back,' she said. 'They're coming along the hard.'

Carrie and Vanessa ran out to the verandah and it was Diane's grey dress they saw first, Diane flying along the hard as if the devil himself was at her heels. Robin was on his way to the stables to feed Rosalind and she saw him at the end of the garden.

'Robbie!' she sobbed. 'Robbie! Thank heaven you're safe!'

She looked at him as if she had brought him up as a good mother should, and the little boy held her at arms' length with a sombre stare.

'I'm going to feed my donkey,' he informed her. 'Would you like to come?'

Diane looked up at the three silent figures on the verandah above her.

'In a minute, darling,' she promised. 'On you go and I'll join you in a minute.'

There was a certain hardness about her expression now, although tears still glistened in her eyes.

'What happened to him?' she demanded. 'Alex

thought I had taken him away.'

'He went on the mountain.' Helena's voice was cold. 'Unfortunately, Max had promised to take him up there one day and he—decided not to wait.'

'But the storm?' Diane protested. 'Was he there alone?'

Helena shook her head.

'Vanessa went after him. She felt that he might have gone up there, by something he said to her.'

Diane turned smouldering eyes in Vanessa's direction.

'Thank you,' she said, but without much gratitude.

Alex had been waylaid by Robin in the garden. They could see his fair head above the hibiscus as he went with his son in the direction of the stables. Wondering what was to happen now, Vanessa turned towards the door to find Carrie's ample figure planted determinedly between her and retreat.

'Helena,' Diane said humbly, 'can I stay?'

The pleading note was, somehow, the most surprising thing. She really did want to stay at La Sola now. Helena stiffened.

'If it's Max you have in mind,' she said harshly, 'the answer is " no ".'

'Max?' Diane's eyes widened in genuine surprise. 'Helena, you don't understand. You never did,' she added with a hint of bitterness. 'I never really loved Max. I was fascinated by something—daring in him, but I never truly loved him. I want my child,' she declared with more determination. 'He needs me.'

'You've taken a long time to think that one out,' Helena retorted sharply.

Diana brushed the soft hair out of her eyes.

'You still don't understand,' she said with amazing calm. 'You hated me from the beginning just because I changed my mind about your favourite son, and you never really tried to get to know me.'

'I know you wrecked Max's life and took Alex from La Sola,' Helena said, but Diane shook her head.

'Alex would never have stayed here,' she declared. 'He wasn't cut out for growing cane and he knew it.

He was like me; he had wider horizons. But that was a long time ago, Helena. We were young and careless then, not much more than children. I knew that I wanted Alex and we went away together. I didn't think till afterwards how it must have hurt Max's pride.'

'His pride!' Helena exclaimed.

'That was all it was, I think. Max would never let a woman spoil his life. He's too strong for that. He would accept it as an unfortunate incident, best forgotten. I didn't mean to hurt anyone,' Diane insisted. 'It was just what I wanted at the time.'

'And now?' Helena demanded, hardly softened by that final confession.

Diane drew a deep breath.

'We must settle this between us, Alex and I.' She was uncertain for the first time in her life. 'We're older and more responsible now, and we have Robin. We must talk together—talk this thing out,' she concluded.

'You can't settle emotions the way you square accounts,' her mother-in-law warned her. 'Feelings don't just balance up that way. If you're doing this solely for the child you'll be making another mistake.'

'I'm not.' Diane turned back towards the garden. 'It's for—all of us. Surely you can see that we're a family—Alex and Robbie and me? We need each other.'

Helena drew herself up to her full height. Her cheeks were deeply flushed but her eyes were calm.

'I'm sorry I never took to you, Diane,' she said, 'but you are Alex's wife and I was willing to settle for that.' Her hands fastened tightly on the verandah rail. 'My grandson has given me a great deal of happiness these past few years, and I'm grateful to you for that. If we have to lose him he will be going to you and Alex and —and I wish you well.'

For a moment Diane stood perfectly still, trying to steady the trembling of her lips. She could not answer Helena now.

'I—have to see Alex,' she whispered as she ran

towards the stables.

Helena sat down heavily on her chair.

'We'll see,' she murmured. 'It will all depend on Alex.' She looked across the verandah to where Vanessa stood beside her sister-in-law. 'What will you do?' she asked.

'I don't know. Alex's book is almost finished and I could get it off to his publisher, even if he wasn't here, or he might want me to take it back to London personally.'

'You're homesick and wanting to leave us?'

'No.' Vanessa had hardly been able to control the tremor in her voice. 'I have no real home any more, but I'll have to find work in London.'

'Are you a city girl?' Helena asked. 'I've never thought so.'

'Of course she isn't!' Carrie declared. 'Any more than you are. This place suits her very well.'

Vanessa felt that her heart must break because those two very dear people were putting into words all the pain she had felt for what seemed to be an eternity. Even parting with warm, good-natured Aunt Carrie would be a wrench, she realised, and she dared not think of Max.

It was over an hour before Diane returned with Alex by her side. Helena had taken up a book and was reading in the long cane chair at the open end of the patio, while Carrie stitched industriously at a dress she was making. She had kept Vanessa talking while she worked mainly because she felt that her sister-in-law needed their moral support.

Alex crossed to his mother's chair, looking diffident.

'Diane and I have been talking things over,' he said.

Helena moved her position to look steadily into his eyes.

'You've made your decision?' she asked.

'Yes.' He drew a deep breath. 'We've come a very long way since—since we agreed to part,' he said. 'We understand each other better now—more fully—but neither of us are cut out for the life at La Sola. I'm sorry, Mother,' he added quickly, 'but that's the way it is. I'm not like Max.'

'No,' Helena agreed. 'Max is like your father.'

'I don't know who I take after,' Alex said ruefully. 'I expect I'm some sort of throwback.'

Helena smiled for the first time.

'You've been successful in your own sphere.' She took a certain amount of pride in his achievements. 'I like to think of you as fulfilled, Alex, but most of all I want to think of you as being happy. A mother wants that for her children more than anything else, and I have Max to look after La Sola. If you must go away again I hope it will not be for so long this time.' She gave him a brave smile. 'Come back,' she invited, 'as often as you can.'

Alex drew Diane forward.

'We'd like to thank you,' he said, 'for all you've done for Robin.'

'He's a delightful child,' Helena answered. 'See that you keep him that way. There's—something of both of you in him.'

If they had expected Diane to kneel at her side and thank her they would have been disappointed, and Vanessa knew that Helena did not want any further show of emotion. Alex and Diane had made their decision and she was glad of it: their marriage had been saved. If she regretted the loss of the little boy she had raised for the past three years she must hide her grief as best she could, although that might be the hardest thing to do when the time came for them to part.

'You're tired,' Carrie said, bending over her chair. 'Maybe you could take your rest now.'

Helena caught her hand, looking up into the plain, craggy face which had seen so much living in fifty-odd years.

'You're good for me, Carrie,' she said gratefully. 'One of these days you and I must talk about settling in the beach house together.'

When they had left her Vanessa went back to her typewriter, trying to concentrate on the work in hand, but unable to shut the thought of her own future out of her mind. Max had not returned from the bay, where he must have seen the yacht and Alex's journey across the Bluff with Diane. The old familiar way; the quickest way back to La Sola! He would know instinctively that they had been united and he was avoiding La Sola in consequence. That was her belief, leading to the conjecture that he still hadn't got over Diane. He did not want to meet her with his brother, to see them for a second time in the full flush of love.

Gritting her teeth, she went back to work, forcing herself to concentrate on Alex's masterpiece. It was a tense, gripping story which held her in spite of her unhappiness, and the author of it had been standing behind her chair for several minutes before she became aware of him.

'I'm sorry,' she apologised. 'I had no idea you'd come in.'

'What were you thinking about?' he asked.

'Your story. It's so true to life, to use an old, hackneyed phrase!'

'I've no intention of changing one line of it,' he declared. 'It must remain as it is and stand or fall on its own merits.'

'It will stand,' she told him. 'You deserve another success.'

He crossed to the edge of the verandah.

'Somehow it doesn't seem to matter so much now,' he said. 'The success and the ballyhoo. They mean very little really when you've faced the loneliness of the damned because you've suddenly realised your mistakes and imagine there's nothing to be done about them. It was a mistake for me to think that Diane was all wrong and I was all right; it was a mistake to allow our miserable existence apart to drag on and on out of pride or pique or what have you, but try telling that to someone like me at the time! As for Diane—' He hesitated, allowing his thoughts to range between the past and the future. 'As for Diane, she's just quietly happy, and that's the most surprising thing of all. The little gay bird has come home to roost.'

Vanessa drew a hard breath.

' At La Sola?' she asked.

He shook his head.

' We're going to Europe. Within striking distance of London, I suppose. Diane has always liked Switzerland, so we'll probably buy a place there, in the sun. There's a school at Lausanne Robin can attend, and then, when he's older, he can finish his education in England.'

' That will please your mother,' Vanessa said, ' especially if you would let him spend part of his holidays here, with her.'

' Of course! He'll never be able to forget the Caribbean, young as he is. Sometimes I think it's in his blood, as it is in Max's.'

' Yes.' She lowered her eyes to the black keys of the typewriter and the page of typescript she had just finished, and all the letters were suddenly blurred as she looked at them. ' Do you want me to go on working on your manuscript?' she asked.

' Why not? I expect you to finish it, even if I won't be here on the auspicious day,' he laughed. ' You can send it off to London for me while I take Diane to Trinidad on our second honeymoon.'

' Why Trinidad?' she managed to ask.

' Because we went there the first time. We sailed right round the island and spent a week at Port of Spain. It was far too hot, of course, but we managed to enjoy it.' He gathered some papers together. ' You're very quiet, Vanessa,' he observed. ' Is there anything wrong?'

She shook her head.

' Nothing. Perhaps I was envying you Port of Spain.'

Their evening meal was a simple one. There were no obvious celebrations, but Diane and Alex looked quietly happy. Half way through, after the chicken Creole had been served, Helena said:

' Max has gone to Antigua. He was called away on business.'

The rather blunt explanation took them all by surprise.

'When was this?' Alex asked.

'Not long after you came home,' Helena said. Alex frowned.

'How long is he likely to be away?' he asked.

'He didn't say.'

'Diane and I had thought of going to Trinidad for a few days.'

'You'll sizzle!' Carrie reminded him.

'I know, but it was a bright idea we had.'

'You go,' Helena said.

'I couldn't—if Max decides to stay away.'

'He won't stay away for long. There's the sugar harvest and a lot more work to do.' Helena looked out at the tropic night. 'He'll be back in a day or two. It was urgent.'

Vanessa could not imagine Max running away for fear of Diane, nor for love of her. Love of La Sola meant as much to him, she thought. Yet a week passed before the schooner put into the bay again. The Schoebergs and the Peranis had sailed away as soon as they had landed Alex and Diane and were probably on their way back to Philadelphia and the bay was deserted save for the schooner. It lay at anchor in its accustomed place, sleek and darkly mysterious as the tropic night descended on the island, leaving only the sounds of carnival to disrupt the peace. The whole island seemed to palpitate to the long notes of drums as the steel bands beat out the rhythm of calypso, and suddenly it was the sound Vanessa knew she would carry away with her and remember for ever.

She turned towards the patio, waiting for Max to come.

'Do you think there's been some trouble in Antigua?' Alex asked as the minutes lengthened and his brother did not appear. 'Perhaps I should go and find out.'

'No, Alex!' Helena put a restraining hand on her son's arm. 'Max will join us in his own good time.'

They were out on the patio, drinking their after-dinner coffee, but it was some time before Max finally strode across the garden to where they sat. His brow was as black as thunder, although he greeted them civilly enough.

'Alex and Diane are going to Port of Spain in the morning,' Carrie informed him. 'If you're taking the schooner across to Bridgetown, I'd like to go with you.'

'I haven't the time,' Max said almost brusquely, 'but you can have the schooner for your trip. Wilson came back with me.'

His expression hadn't changed as he looked in Diane's direction, but he seemed to be seeing her now from a great distance.

'We'd have to wait till Thursday for the freighter,' Alex pointed out.

'There's no need for you to wait,' Max said. 'The schooner will be lying idle for at least a week while we celebrate the sugar harvest.'

'Yes,' Alex said. 'I'd forgotten.' He turned to his wife. 'Would you like to stay for Carnival, Diane?'

'I'd rather go to Trinidad.' She smiled up at him, sure of his response. 'Wouldn't you?'

'Need you ask?' He kissed her on the tip of the nose. 'Trinidad it is!'

This must be awful for Max, Vanessa thought, but when she looked in his direction after a while she imagined that he was just angry. Pain or anger, what did it matter? Perhaps a man was able to substitute anger for pain after a while.

Alex left very few instructions before he left on his 'second honeymoon', but perhaps he had said all he had to say about the finishing of her task. When the typescript was safely despatched to London there would be nothing for her to do, nothing in Switzerland and nothing here. He probably wouldn't start to write again for another year.

A whole year! She thought about those intervening months with a sense of dread until she knew that she should go, even before Alex returned. If his book was finished and despatched to London he would perhaps understand how she felt. Better to go quickly when the time came than prolong the agony of seeing Max day after day steeped in this mood of angry silence, waiting for the end of Carnival so that he could sail away once more into the blue forgetfulness of the sea.

The schooner returned from Barbados two days later. Alex and Diane had flown from Bridgetown to Port of Spain, taking Robin with them, and they would not be back for over a week.

Typing furiously, Vanessa finished the MS and parcelled it up to send it to England with a covering letter to Alex's publishers. There would be little doubt about its reception, she felt, conscious of a small thrill of pride at the part she had played during its birth. Alex would go on to greater things now, always with Diane by his side. He didn't need to pretend any more.

Towards the end of the week she told Helena that she must go.

'Why?' Helena looked up at her with a shock of surprise in her eyes.

'There's nothing left for me to do.'

'Because Alex has gone?' Helena looked perturbed, searching her face for the truth.

'No, not that.'

'What, then?'

'I have no claim on La Sola. My work for Alex is finished.'

'Stay,' Helena urged. 'You're needed here.'

Vanessa looked away.

'How can I?' she cried. 'How can I stay?'

Helena did not argue the point. It was the final night of Carnival and they were expected to be there. Down in the village all the signs of revelry were already in evidence, the gay lanterns slung from the trees, the paraffin flares marking out the dirt road and ringing the hard, the laughter and gaiety, the bright kaleidoscope of colour moving ceaselessly to the rhythm of calypso under a tropic moon. It was more than Vanessa could bear to look at, yet she had no excuse to offer Helena when they were ready to go.

Carrie and Helena sat in special chairs in front of the crowd, with a cool little wind fanning their cheeks

186

as it came in across the lagoon. The schooner still lay in the bay, but there was no sign of Max. Perhaps he did not mean to come, although he would be expected to put in an appearance at this exotic harvest-home.

When the dancing began in earnest there was little time for thought or conjecture. The compelling rhythm of calypso directed their feet on to the wooden floor beneath the palms, and Vanessa found herself joining in the revelry, passed from one to another of the estate overseers until, suddenly, she was in Max's arms.

'So you're leaving?' he said brusquely.

'Yes.' There's nothing else for me to do.'

'When?' She felt the pressure of his arms until it seemed she could hardly breathe.

'If I could go over with the schooner next time it's going to Bridgetown I could book my air passage back to England from there.'

'Without seeing Alex to say good-bye?'

'I think we've said our good-byes.'

Her voice faded into the sound of calypso. She could see Max's face in the light from the flares, with no kindness in it, but they danced on. The music washed over her, threatening to drown her senses as she listened to its insistent beat. It was like being swept by a current far out to sea, out to that warm, silky Caribbean whose waves had lulled her into a sense of security on more than one occasion. Treacherous, beautiful Caribbean, exotic mirror of so much heartache and so much joy!

When the time came for them to return to La Sola, she walked back to the house with Carrie Hazeltine.

'I'm sorry you're going, Vanessa,' Carrie said. 'We've grown very fond of you in those few short weeks.'

'I know.' Vanessa could hardly utter the words. 'You've all been so very, very kind. I'll never forget La Sola, but the job I came to do is finished.'

'You won't go on working for Alex?' Carrie seemed surprised.

'No. This was only a temporary job.'

'There's Diane, of course,' Carrie mused. 'She'll keep him from writing as much as he did.'

'A novelist has to relax some time!'

'So it would seem.' They had reached the garden and Carrie sighed. 'I had hoped Helena would come to the beach house,' she said. 'It would be easier for her there than up here on the edge of the Bluff, but she won't leave La Sola till Max takes a wife.'

'Do you think he ever will?' Vanessa asked, her heart beating fast.

'Who's to say?' Carrie turned at the foot of the verandah steps. 'We rather thought—'

What had been thought was left for the night to discover. With an added sigh, Carrie trudged up the wooden steps as Max came up behind them with his mother.

'Good-night,' he said when they were all in the sitting-room. 'We've seen all there is to see of Carnival for another year.'

Helena was most reluctant to part with Vanessa.

'I'll miss you,' she said, again and again, 'and so will Max. You have been more than a help to us both.'

A help, Vanessa thought. She did not want to be a help to Max merely because she could relieve him of a burden of paperwork, and if that was all she could ever be she was prepared to go.

The schooner was sailing to Barbados the following day to pick up Alex and Diane and she made ready to go with it. She would say good-bye to Alex in Bridgetown.

Wondering who would captain the *Carmelita*, she was prepared for Wilson, but it was Max who stood on deck, waiting. Her suitcases, packed hastily the night before, were slung into the launch which closed the gap to the schooner's side in an incredibly short space of time. She dared not look back towards the lagoon, nor would she turn her eyes towards the Bluff where Max had first warned her of danger.

How long ago that seemed now!

He helped her on to the deck. There was a stiff

wind blowing and the *Carmelita* bowed before it, her white sails spread like wings, her bowsprit dipping rhythmically as she breasted the little waves and made for the open sea.

It was no day to go below as the trade wind blew steadily over the quarter and the siren song of the rigging filled the air with adventurous sound. She looked round for Max and found him leaning back against the rail beside her, his dark face upturned to the sky.

'Why are you going?' he demanded. 'My mother asked you to stay.'

'But not you, Max!' She turned to face him. 'I could never stay without you wanting me at La Sola.'

'Wanting you!' The wind seemed to shout an echo to his words. 'I've wanted you since I first saw you, over there in Bridgetown.' His voice was harsh and taut with emotion. 'I was stupid enough to think that you were Alex's property, though, and mad enough with rage to believe that I had the right to take you from him. Then I discovered that it didn't matter any more. Diane was dead as far as I was concerned, dead and buried.' All the tension seemed to go out of him with the words and he was smiling when he said: 'Supposing I should fulfil my role as pirate and tell you that I'm not taking you to Barbados?'

'Max—!'

He smothered her protest with a kiss.

'What would you say?' he demanded.

'I'd rather you took me home to La Sola,' she told him quietly. 'Your mother will want to know.'

'That we're being married,' he said. 'Yes, I think she will, although I have half a notion that she already has it fixed in her mind. When I had to rush off to Antigua the other day she told me I ought to keep you on the island.'

'Why did you go?' Vanessa asked, indifferent now to the thought of Diane. 'You seemed so angry.'

'Black with rage, in fact,' he laughed. 'It had nothing to do with Diane or La Sola or you.' His brows drew together again, but his arm was still about her. 'It had something to do with getting rid of the old piratical image, I suppose. Nick Milford was shipping contraband on one of my yachts out of Antigua and they were waiting for him in Haiti. I couldn't let that go on and do nothing about it, or even be blamed for turning a blind eye. At one time it wouldn't have mattered to me, but—' He held her face up for his kiss. 'It does now,' he concluded.

They sailed on to Barbados, after all. It was one thing to talk of piracy on the deep seas and quite another to fall down on a promise.

They met Alex and Diane and Robin off the plane from Trinidad.

'We're not at all surprised,' Alex said when he heard their news. 'Welcome to the family, Vanessa.'

Robin was first to board the schooner.

'I'll have to get back quick to see Rosalind,' he decided. 'She must be a lonely donkey without me.'

Max put his arm about his future wife.

'There would have been a lot of loneliness at La Sola, if things had been different,' he said.

The trade wind blew them home to the island, a gentle trade wind with warmth in its breath, and when they came level with the lagoon they could see Carrie and Helena on the shore, walking towards the beach house, which Carrie had prepared for them so long ago.

'This is what she wanted,' Max said as the distant figures stopped to wave. 'To end her days at the beach house with Carrie while I brought my wife back to the plantation house up there on the the ridge. It's an old tradition, Vanessa. The island is full of tradition, but this one is ours for the keeping.'

As the schooner's anchor rattled down into the translucent water of the bay Vanessa knew how true that was.

'It will be kept, with love, always in my heart,' she said, watching the launch as it sped from the jetty to meet them.